INGRESS

LAVANYA SHANIVARSANTHE

INDIA • SINGAPORE • MALAYSIA

ISBN 979-8-89186-766-6

For

Aaradhya, who is more of a teacher to me than I am a mother to her.

Contents

Ingress

"You cannot be my blood!" his father's remarks reverberated in Dodari's ears. As they carried him on the bamboo stretcher through the forest, his brothers, two older and two younger, had jeered at him, "Can't you kill a simple wild boar? It's not like father's days when an elephant had to be killed for the ingress!", "The hunter became the hunted" and "What kind of a soldier are you!" That was all last week when a wild boar, a mother wild boar, had struck him down, injuring his hip, limbs and ankle. In the following days, the monsoons had engulfed the entire landscape. Dodari, despite his injury and the monsoons, had gone to the forest to hunt on all those days. But he had failed.

Dodari and the tribe to which he belonged had lived on the fringes of the forest, just like all his ancestors did. But now, what had been a habitat historically had taken the form of a village; what with the borders being drawn and maps being put on paper by the government. The village was adjacent to the K-colony, a new settlement brought by the government for building a hydroelectric plant on what the tribals claimed to be *their* river. Dodari's people were disgruntled as the land was always theirs, and with the forming of the K-colony, the government was bringing people from all around the state. So, when Dodari left the tribe to join the army, he was not surprised that they began treating him like an outcast. However, when the government built some concrete houses for all the villagers, they mellowed down.

Today's forecast said it was going to be a clear day, but the wetness somehow managed to linger on his dry bed as he sat waiting for the sun to show. He caressed his ankle with the oil his mother used when she was alive. His wounds seemed healed almost completely now. All the wetness of the week's rain soaked into his metaphorical brain, and moisture seeped through his downturned, droopy eyes. His used, tender feet felt like dead mollusks that were caught under his bare steps; and his calves' felt like blood-sucking leeches, all having partook in *that* hunting expedition. He wiped his calves in jitters.

The stridulations of the night insects were long dead and soon made way for a pair of early birds. He decided to go for the hunt as soon as the sun divulged his intentions, as he had done in the last few days. For, the Sun was God. He looked out the window again, avoiding meeting eyes with anyone else before he prayed the sun. To see the sun first thing in the morning brought good fortune. Even while training for the army, he had looked for the sun first, avoiding faces and eyes between the morning call and sunrise. It was when he was waiting for his first posting after the end of training, that he had received an emergency call to return to his village, to fulfill the wish of his dying old man – the wish to die a peaceful death. The wish to get a rite of passage into heaven, which was possible only after the ingress of all of his sons into the tribe. And for that to happen, each of them had to kill a wild boar and display his mettle to the tribe. His two older brothers and the two younger brothers had accomplished this. After the ingress, the two older brothers had married, and the younger ones couldn't marry despite their ingress as Dodari, being older than them, was yet to prove himself.

Soon, the sun spread himself in the sky. Dodari stood against the mullions of the window and looked up with folded hands. He readied his hunting gear, not forgetting *the* spear with which his brothers had teased him. The structure of their house was at the crux of confusion. It was a motley of reconstructions desperately trying to accommodate the advancements of technology on the one hand and an unrelenting old man who tried to retain the sentiments of the old home on the other. As he stood at the door leading to the street, he heard his father's coarse, muffled voice, almost begging him, "Please kill a wild boar! Send me to the doors of heaven! Please!"

It was the first time Dodari had seen his father speak so. His eyes were yellow from the unrelenting jaundice. The hardened bed smelled of his urine and had stains of yellow. Spots of red seemed to spread rapidly in his eyes. None of the others had slept all night as the old man's condition had deteriorated further. And the shaman was relentlessly trying to keep him alive.

"I can do it in a heartbeat with a gun," Dodari was astonished to feel some sympathy for the old man.

"Heavens don't use guns at its doorway," he turned away and closed his eyes.

"How long do you want to live this life of shame?" his youngest brother said, flashing his tattoo of a boar he had gotten after his kill and entry into the pride. All his brothers had one, some on their arms and some on their thighs, which clearly showed below their loincloths. Dodari ignored his brothers and walked out.

"It was a cloudy day! Sun was not in favor," Dodari unhinged a smile to the shaman, who was grinding some forest herbs on the porch. The eldest snatched the spear from behind him and began teasing his loincloth and misfortune. Again.

"Don't forget Saroo," another winked. Oh, he had forgotten about Saroo. The most beautiful girl, or so they said in the tribe. But for Dodari, she was just another girl. Uncouth and uncivilized in her ways just like his brothers. Ever since his inception into the army, she acted funny around him. Her father had droopy eyes just like him and he remembered having thought it was good that she had not inherited those eyes. She had brought him fruits and warm food all week when he was ill. "That girl who whiles away all her time under the big tree?" Dodari snatched the spear right back.

"Five days have passed. Every morning you head out with the same gear and return empty-handed. At least pick some of Father's favorite roots and berries on your way today," another said from behind a stack of harvest bags. "That way you will have done some kind of service to him."

"The laws of the state have changed and so has the virility of you man-boys," the old man said between his thrusting coughs. And then, lifting his head up from the pillow, he said faintly to Dodari, "I always knew you were the most useless of my sons. I knew it the moment I saw you." As Dodari exited the house, the old man cried to the shaman sourly, "Pour him some drugs to increase his competency!"

The early morning air intermixed with the fresh smells of the cow dung cakes smeared on the walls for fuel by the women. After walking on the highway, Dodari took a wide, empty pathway that led to a grove and from there headed east where the forest turned very dense. His tall, recently chiseled body cut a sharp figure and cast a long shadow against the morning sun. His droopy eyes looked unwilling and half awake. When outside the village, he always wore modern clothes like everyone else. And back in the village, he tied a blue gingham loincloth and a messy turban on his head. Just like everyone else. He was the only one in his family and the first one in his tribe to have gone out and made something of himself. His sense of direction was acclaimed not only in his village but even in the neighboring villages. Everyone said, "Even the ghosts of our ancestors could get lost in the forest but not Dodari. The sun speaks to him."

But according to Dodari, it was not a very difficult course. "One must not postulate the idea of it. If you did, your heart trips and your mind will play tricks," he told everyone, "And Look! Look, and the sun will show you." There had been 2 or 3 points in the route where others got confused and took a wrong turn. Like he said, *postulation.* The first one was a small boulder that served as a pointer. But sometimes, from the little landslides nearby, little rocks covered it up, misguiding even seasoned hunters. The second pointer was near a small gorge where the varying seasonal water levels changed the entire landscape. And finally, at the last pointer, where all the small streams of rivers merged and where the direction was sought from the sound of the mighty river, the echoes from the surrounding hillocks befogged the brains. If one lost at any one of these pointers he was a goner. It was grand, his sense of direction, but eventually, the fame got assimilated into his person, even taken for granted and the time came when questions rose about his ingress into the tribe, which became pertinent as his father was the head of the tribe as well.

Once inside the forest, Dodari was at ease, like a child in his mother's lap. No ray of light escaped the canopies, and for long stretches, he couldn't feel the presence of the sun. Only the wet forest floor prevailed; the detritus struggling to dry up despite the clear skies of the last couple of days. Every now and then, he looked at the sky for looming clouds, near and far in the direction he was heading. He observed their patterns and sizes and what they meant for the rest of his plan. When he reached the row of springs that rushed and gushed, he washed his face, arms, and cleared the mud off his feet. Fresh as a flower, he sang announcedly, slapping his plain, bare thighs and whistling in between –

Onward and forward, Dodari
For the sun is smiling today,
The light is aligned and gay.

Onward and forward, Dodari
For you know what others not know,
Way to the valley where boars go.

Onward and forward, Dodari
For the clouds have scattered away
To the might of the sun's ray.

Onward and forward Dodari,
For the play of the shadow –
Is a path for you to endow.

Onward and forward, Dodari
This tryst will end in a win –
And put an end to your brothers' sin.

By the time Dodari reached the valley, the sun was up on his head and began playing games with the flirtatious clouds. He walked further east to reach a vast grassland that was burdened with defeated silver grass. Heaps of it stood drooping from the heavy hand of the week's rainfall. The wild boars were known to wander here in high numbers. Across the mountains, he could see the river and streams in full life. A mild wind brought with it the quenched relish of the wild animals, and the stench of degrading, left-over bones and animal parts. He crossed the tall grasses and sat on the other side where the wind did not bring any odor of the decaying flesh. *If only I could borrow the gun from the headman and get a kill, it would all be over in a jiffy*, he thought. The conundrum of his father's entry into hell or heaven will be resolved. He began to send out cries of boars, as he walked on the edge of the grassland. He decided to get down to the river and set a trap if no game resulted in these grasslands. The sun was still high up and intense and he felt optimistic.

When he had walked half the perimeter of the grassland, heavy clouds trespassed unexpectedly into the terrain and threw itself over the grassland like a blanket. The howling clouds began to give him a running sweat, making him want to catch a breath. He sat down on a peculiar-looking log infested with algae. It had no business being there. *Maybe an elephant brought it from the other side*, he thought. He sang a song his mother had taught him

All of the hunters are dead –
Dead with the elephants they killed;
Leaving the rest to nurture,
Nurture that –
which the dead left for the future.

He gazed around. Everything behind him was still, green and wet. There was no disturbance. If he got it right today, the approbation would be his alone. And the solvency would merit and sit well in front of the entire tribe. And of course, the ingress, however irrelevant in the modern times. In front of him was the path that led to the river below. He sent out cries again. Behind his superfluent optimism lingered on the sight of the cloud he had caught beside the sun earlier in the day. As he sat there, questions arose as to what his eyes had caught first in the morning. The sun and the clouds had existed alongside each other. *The bloody clouds!* They struck his mind like a quirk and popped every now and then, bothering him, tossing his optimism every now and then. He sipped some alcohol to calm his nerves.

He began walking again, now hiding in the dense albeit known paths, and continued giving out calls in desperation more frequently. After a while he mellowed on the calls, realizing that desperation came in all languages. On the other hand, he felt a sense of power and high-headedness as he alone knew to navigate these areas.

He checked on his weapons. They were alright. Then, he noticed a mass of something gray. He threw himself down to hide. Was it moving? He waited to see if it moved. It did, and it had a head. It was a young boar, seemingly lost, but it was making the most by trying to scour for food in the grass. He found something and began to chew on it.

Staring into nothing, it seemed like it was trying to decide which path to take to get back to its passel. Dodari did not move, but only held his head above the horizon of the grass. His heart pranced in excitement. This was an easy catch and he did not want to mess it up. *A baby boar*! He knew how his brothers would jeer at him again. But if he killed it, the older ones would come looking for it. So, he decided to set a trap. The drooping grassland made visibility better, and for the first time, he felt thankful for the rains of last week.

The young boar, easily distracted, continued to grunt and scout the marshy ground for dirt and all that was edible in the thickets. Dodari decided to wait for the sun to appear from behind the clouds, for everything *must* go well. And he hoped, in the meanwhile, the boar would move to a vantage point. He slowly sat down on the wet leaves, his eyes following the boar as it moved naively at leisure, without exercising any caution.

Dodari had barely slept or eaten in the last week and the alcohol made him a bit drowsy and susceptible. He crouched down a bit to gather himself, shook his head and squeezed his eyes. When he felt better, he looked up. The boar was gone. He panicked and began to send out grunt calls which he had learned from his brothers, forming a downwind position. The calls were in short bursts. He waited, sent out calls again, and repeated this until he sensed the insincerity in his calls. He stopped and sat disappointed. The boar should have come running out of the thicket within a matter of seconds had his calls been candid. He gave up and headed in the possible direction of the boar. His spirit was doused in failure. After much walking, he reached a small grove and there, he saw it again! It was tending to a laceration. He alerted himself.

"*It's so weak in its hind legs, I can see it trembling,*" he thought as he cleared the water from the corner of his eyes. *This is my kill!* He bent his body over the ground, his bare chest almost grazing the ground as he moved. The familiar smell of the murky leaves filled his nostrils. *One step at a time, you don't want to catch its attention now!* Never had he reached so close and so alone to a wild boar. He moved his hand surreptitiously and reached out to the spear. His happiness knew no bounds as he neared it.

He walked slowly and measuredly and just when he was nearing his kill, he stepped on an aperture of dry leaves, and from beneath it came *Psssss...Psss....* His heart stopped and he turned to look at the pig which was now staring straight at the tree under which he stood. He held his breath and did not blink an eye. With just a few meters between them, Dodari could hear the boar alternating between breathing and grunting. They had both locked eyes and the boar seemed to question his tenacity to do anything beyond this point. He took an offensive stance with his spear raised to his elbow, like the warriors in the cave paintings, a lesson his ancestors had passed on through blood.

At that moment, again *Hissss...Pshissss.* A snake! His heart pounded as he slowly moved his feet. *Hisss...Hissss...* The boar looked at him questioningly. From the corner of his eyes, Dodari saw a pit viper not far from where he stood. It was slithering around, revelling in the leaves and vaguely heading towards him. *It is not venomous!* Time slowed down as it charged onward, making its way across the heap of leaves leisurely. Its colors changed under the glaring sun or so he thought. *Am I hallucinating?*

"I am not scared of snakes," he hissed to both the animals in anguish. He was. He decided to stay still as it was the only way to get through this. However, the snake decided to shift a bit and settled thoroughly on Dodari's feet. The boar got back to nursing its lacerations. Its neglect for his presence left Dodari enraged.

"I have had enough of all this!" he rumbled and just as he positioned himself to leap on the boar, the sun came out and almost immediately sent a lightning flash from the spear onto the eyes of the boar. And like a deer, it sprung to attack Dodari. Dodari tripped on a small stone, his ankle twisted and the direction of his flying spear changed. The dumb animal, scared of its own sudden leap, turned around only to get struck by the unintended spear. He ran a few meters and dropped into the bushes behind the rows of eucalyptus trees.

Dodari's torso collapsed onto the ground, as he watched in a haze, his eyes still watery. His feet were numb and began to exert gravity on his body. Sweat entered his eyes and burned them further. "Oh, Lord Sun! What are your ways?" He was shivering and a strange resentment filled him. He put the dead boar into a gunny bag he had been carrying and began to walk towards the village. He sang to keep himself from worrying about the impending ridicule of having killed just a baby boar.

***

The sharp, evening sun shone right into his eyes when he entered the village. A strange unknown satisfaction filled him. A satisfaction that was not his, but his father's. He carried the gunny bag in his right hand and another white cotton bag in his left. People had gathered outside his house, casting long shadows that all merged and overlapped on one another. But not enough people to presume that the old man was dead. *If he is dead, he died at the time of the boar,* he thought.

"Where the hell were you?" one of his older brothers came running. Dodari thought he would get thrashed, but did not.

"To the forest of course. Is he dead?"

"He will not die until he has seen a dead boar! He is wheezing under his breath and waiting for your return."

"Did you kill?" Saroo asked from the sidelines.

"Yes." Dodari turned to his brothers to read their faces.

The oldest said gravely, "Come, let him learn of his place in heaven."

"He's losing his mind, let him see it with his own eyes for peace. There's no one but him to be convinced of the ingress of his sons," the shaman said.

With blood dripping from its corner, Dodari pulled the dead boar from the gunny bag and held it high. Someone shook the old man who was awake but out of sorts. With his yellow, red-spotted eyes batting rapidly, and a voice overtaken by obsession, he looked up to catch sight of that on which his entire life now culminated. A precipice. A make or break.

The golden sunlight fell on the dangling boar through the row of mullions. The old man, his yellow eyes filled with a final hope, stared at it for a moment in scatters and finally grunted, "What have you brought? What is this striped, yellow creature?! You thought this is a boar?!" He yelled gathering all his angst. He then turned to Dodari with big, raging eyes and trembling hands, trying to grab his arms, and said, "I knew it the moment I set my eyes on you…" he gasped for more anger, but fell dead with a thud on the yellow-stained bed.

The air filled with the remains of the dead.

"Will he enter hell or heaven?" the youngest one asked the shaman.

GREEN

Saroo is called the most beautiful girl in the village. She came of age last year and her parents have been looking for a suitor. When they said they do not mind looking for a boy from the colony, Saroo protested vehemently that if she ever married, it would be a man from her tribe. A rare desire as all the other girls of the tribe wanted to marry an "outside man" so that they could leave the village and live a better life.

Saroo lay down on the grass under the banyan tree in the grove. It was *her* tree; *My big tree,* she called it. Her grandmother cleared out weeds from around the bushes of herbs she was growing in a small patch right next to the big tree.

Staring at the clear, blue sky, Saroo thought about the day Dodari walked past that same grove to kill the boar. She wished she had talked to him that day, when instead, she had gotten up hurriedly and hid behind the tree. Dodari had not noticed her, but she watched him go about, worried about his kill. *I would have distracted him*, she thought. Despite having not spent much time with him, she longed for his company, like she longed for her big tree every morning. The big tree rustled for attention. "Oh, what do you know!" Saroo whispered and blushed.

The sky was getting sharper by the minute, awash in the afternoon sun. Growing up, the trees were Saroo's friends as she sat down each day, waiting for her grandmother to finish picking up roots and herbs and occasionally, a game; just like today. The fluttering of the leaves were her conversations and she saw acumen in the way the big tree chose to grew its branches. As she sat for hours under various trees, she analyzed them - from root hairs to the last of its leaves. Of the lot, the big tree was her favorite; and she thought it was more than a thousand years old. It quivered at the slightest kiss of the wind and danced a thousand dances. It was a wonder, how such a thing of immobility could dance a thousand dances; the more it danced the more she was enticed. "Why are the leaves green?" she asked her grandmother. "There's so much of them! Is it green beyond the forest too?"

"You have been asking that question for so long now," her grandmother said between her breaths as she squatted and pulled out the weeds, throwing them all into a pile in a corner. "I think it's time for you to learn the saga of the green forest. It will answer all your questions…"

Long ago, there was a Mother Tree. When Mother Tree decided to dance, nobody could stop her. The wish to dance was considered peculiar and almost taboo by the rest of them. Mother Tree stood tall and colorless at the center of the Tectonic Plate below her, further surrounded by knolls and mounds. Her primary purpose was to procreate and fill the land with her offsprings, the Children Trees. It was her destiny. And in doing so, over the years, she had formed mountain ranges over the bigger knolls and mounds. All the trees across the land were translucent and chose to be so in order to avoid attacks by the evil spirits who, the Mother Tree worried, would hinder her procreation. She wanted to fill all of the land with trees and more trees, make a home to the blue and yellow subjects. Her trunk was enormous, expansive and her branches had a discipline and mind of their own – growing out and around the trunk in regularity like a danseuse – rhythmic at a left, a notch above and a right, a step back and then one at the front, a step forward and again one at the back. During intermittent spells of silence, you could listen to her songs and see her swanning like a mystic. The Children Trees ran all around her, all in all, embedded like a giant, dense network of gossamer, but only so complex and convoluted that there was no demarcation between them. This deep, enormous root system clutched onto the Tectonic Plate, and around it ran a winding, unbridled stream that always tended to the trees.

The Tectonic Plate was wise and old and had seen everything since the beginning of time. He was called the Elderly. The Mother Tree too obliged him during matters of conflict and so did the Lords.

Lord of Blue was the Ocean. He was to the west of the mountain ranges and had established a fiduciary relationship with all of his blue subjects over time. Rows of corn flowers, bluebells, and blue hyacinths, clouded by bushy blueberry plants, were home to families of blue jays, buntings, swallows, and western and eastern bluebirds, all formed thickets at the foothills of the mountain ranges. Blue sea stars, poison dart frogs, blue crabs, and royal blue tangs all dwelled in the Ocean himself. Similarly, the Sun established his kingdom over all the yellows. Dandelions, daffodils, corn fields, goldfinches, crab spiders, honeycombs and bumblebees swarmed the forests and the foothills.

However, there were no borders. In the mornings, when the Sun shone on the Mother Tree, she glowed like a golden armor, basking in it and transforming into a pellucid source of yellow radiance. And with dusk, she took the darkness of the blue night, nestling hundreds of blue jays and blue morphos that retreated into her bosom. Everyone lived freely and worked around their jobs in the ecosystem.

Mother Tree sat on the fence in matters of the cold war between the Lords. There was hearsay about a war that happened much before she came into being but none talked about it out of fear of the Lords. She declared she would stay out of it and that she just wanted to dance when the wind blew and procreate.

As days passed, her frequent dances were making the old Tectonic Plate unstable. There was a deliberation when the Tectonic Plate said the mountain ranges were now full and there was no need for further procreation and that she could rest. They had become so thick and dense that the dances of the Mother Tree sent out heavy reverberations across the entire Tectonic Plate and it was all getting too much to handle. But the Mother Tree protested that she had found true happiness in dancing and was not willing to stop what made her happy. She was only recovering from an illness; a plague-like illness that affected her trunk and leaves. Her trunk shrank and her colorless leaves turned brittle, shattering at the slightest touch. In order to protect her children from catching the plague she began to shake off herself to rid herself of all the affected leaves and they shattered into the streams and then flowed into the Ocean. But in this process of dancing, the Mother Tree began to heal because she enjoyed it and it brought her happiness. After much back and forth, and much pleading by her, they reached an understanding that she would dance only when the westerlies came calling. The Mother Tree loved dancing so much she couldn't wait and began to dance much before the westerlies arrived. She did so stealthily. But there was no deceiving the wise Tectonic Plate, for her dancing sent out reverberations of geographical proportions. He warned her, but the Mother Tree did not pay heed.

On a fine cloudless day, the Tectonic Plate sat down with the Mother Tree and asked her, "Has anyone ever told you of the story of the formation of the knolls and mounds, on which you have spread so extensively now?"

"No."

"This was much before you sprouted from the enchanted, crystalline seed. It was the era of the Sun's gravitational dances. There were Hell Ants. Ferocious little things. They snapped their scythe-like mandibles to catch prey. They eventually enjoyed it so much that they began to form little armies to dig the land beneath in unison. The sounds of it became so strong that it sent out shock waves. They began to make heaps and heaps of soil, pebbles, rocks, the mounds became much greater in height than the ant hills. I appealed to the Lords, and the Sun offered to make peace, but the Ants, blinded in their confidence, began to speak highly of their united strength, that they were invincible. They decided to stand up to the Sun and Ocean and said they wanted to become the third Lord. The Sun, in a glaring action, sent out a whiplash of solar flare and in a single beat assimilated the entire army. That's how the mounds remained in the state they are today, and in smaller heights. The Ocean let his streams run around them to cover up any signs of a war. You can see the remnants and craters under the stream even to this day."

"So, it is true! When the streams ran about singing songs of the war that gave birth to them, I thought it was all in merry. I did not know the gory details behind it."

"I am the oldest and wisest and my apostolic survival is very essential for the survival of this land. You must understand."

The Mother Tree understood the subtle threat and it was valid too. Her dancing was disturbing an equilibrium. And equilibrium was paramount.

The Mother Tree laid low for a few days to appease the Tectonic Plate. But as summer came to an end, she couldn't hold any longer. Happiness became habitual. And with it came dancing. She tried to restrict the dancing to the nights, but the Tectonic Plate never slept and continued to warn her.

As summer came to an end, she decided to dance no matter what. For, all her life she had to be selfless, but now she wanted to do a bit of something for herself and that was to dance and not just to the tunes and beats of the westerlies. So she did, springing her branches to left and right and swirling to her back as much as she could. The leaves that once felt brittle, quivered in joy again, prancing up and down, bending their selves in romance to the sides like a shy bride. A thousand dances accorded and rhythm penetrated deep in her soul.

All this the Mother Tree did when night struck. When the knolls, the mounds, her own children, the mountain, the stream that connected with the Ocean at the end of sight, all slept. But nothing escaped the Tectonic Plate. He was beginning to get displaced and it grew him anxious and anguished. He convened a meeting with the Sun and the Ocean and decided to go all out. The uncalled desire of the

Mother Tree to dance was called out as outrageous. It was a taboo. It was neither in its nature nor clause. Moreover, she had been granted her westerlies stint only as an exception, for dancing improved the survival rates of her children. Moreover, this was not even necessary at this stage.

The early morning news enraged the forces of nature. The Sun was accommodative and willing to talk about it. He supported the Mother Tree, but the Ocean bellowed, sending waves of destruction. Mother Tree was emboldened by the support of the Sun. And with her peculiar desire now outed, she went all out too. She would dance and nobody dared stop her! "I have given and given, treated you all like my own children. I have offered shelter, propagated the directional cause of the wind, held the soil in my roots, and given vegetation to the barren mounds and shade to the marine life that runs in the streams. All my life has been spent away, now I want to do something for myself!"

Her defiance was received with a rancid taste. And under this pretext, the cataclysmic cold fight between the Sun and the Ocean now surfaced. The Sun being the supreme of yellows gave a war call to the yellows. The Ocean who long wanted to be the supreme rallied all the blues. In actuality, the Ocean neither supported the Mother Tree nor discouraged it. But he was not willing to let go of this chance to establish supremacy.

And thus, a second war of might became imminent. By noon, everyone assembled. The yellows harangued about the need to preserve the sanctity, the need to respect what was and what was to be, to respect the tenets of everything that was. The yellow daffodils burst out in a moment's notice, filling everything around it yellow – the soil, the fringes of the stream, the foot of the tree trunks and even the base of the Mother Tree, almost encroaching her. The crab spiders changed dramatically from white to yellow and circled and strung around the Mother Tree and with their hunting cries added yellow to the leaves. The bumblebees lined up, creating a buzzing harmony, almost shielding the Sun itself with their swarms of amazing but hostile patterns reminding the blues how they suffered their sting in the first war. Their color cousins, the hover flies formed a second line of defense behind them, and so did the ambush bugs, hiding in plain sight on the scaffoldings formed by the daffodils on land and water lilies in the streams. The streams that joined the Ocean became part of the Ocean's army, while the stream under the aegis of the Mother Tree, began to reflect the sunlight, forming a firmament of blinding lights against the blues. A maelstrom of fire salamanders began to produce the neurotoxins on its toxic skin glands and nestled in the pile of mosses, rocks and logs for camouflage. They were the sniper team. The golden shield lichens spread like wildfire all over the Mother Tree. So did the yellow aphids.

The Mother Tree stood tumultuous and bewildered at the bizarre discipline the Lords had over their subjects. The Ocean's nerves cracked, and he went wild looking at this army of yellows encroaching the Mother Tree. His anger altered the gravitational pull and down came crashing a verdigris meteor and everything turned blue in a matter of seconds. The crests and troughs pranced high. Those who added the blues were adding the blues and became angry when lichens and aphids spread. Blue oozed into the leaves where the yellows had taken a foothold. The Sun, in his signature move, sent out whiplashes of a hundred solar flares, lighting up the entire sky. And everything went blind. All that was warring mixed and intermixed and turned into a new color onto the Mother Tree, melting under the heat and splashing itself all over the land. A green pigment came into being. When everything settled, the Mother Tree woke up to the chirps and buzzes of surviving creatures and vowed never to disturb the balance of nature again. As a mark of respect for the Lords, and to keep her word to the Tectonic Plate, she changed the colors of her leaves every changing season and shed them to give new life. She warded off the evil forces for several years, until little creatures called humans came along.

A strong wind blew. Saroo got up and danced along with the leaves of *her* big tree.

THE KING WILL SEE YOU NOW

When summer came, we all headed to the estate. *Our* estate. It was in faraway Nettana, a village where my father was born. As for my father, it was an antiquated desire of an ancestor who had died brooding over his fraudulently lost patch of land—a coffee plantation, to be specific. In order to fulfill that desire, he purchased an estate last year, using a lot of savings. All year he has been moping over two matters. The first, an unfulfilled dream of having a son, which he frequently blamed on Mother for not trying for a second child. And second, how the estate is going to be his home once he retires from his government post in the colony. He has even designated a burial place next to this "home".

But, exhaustion soon set in when a realization dawned upon him that it was not all fun and frolic to nurture a plantation. To add to the worries, a treading path cut open the plantation like a demon's mouth, dividing it into a lakeside, which was one-quarter, and a highway side, three-quarters, leading to a roundabout fencing, sprinkler setup resulting in an unattended pique that was accumulating every day in labor and resource handling. A lot of scattered wandering was happening as it was the end of the harvest cycle. And to top it all, they had decided to process the cherries before selling them, unlike every year when the cherries were sold directly after picking. So, there was neither the time nor the fervor to press on a "survival exposure".

On the last day of our high school, the headmistress had walked into our class to bid adieu. After a rather moving speech, she'd said, "I'm assigning a task for you all. Something to keep your minds engaged for the summer and before you all start college. Of course, I cannot force it on you, but I believe, after all these years, I can trust you all to take it upon yourselves to complete this assignment. Perhaps you can share the essays amongst yourselves." She then gave the topic—*Life Skills*. She did not give any pointers. Maybe she thought if she did it would cause some kind of intellectual hindrance to us. Some of my friends decided to write about the camping and hiking trips they were about to take. One said she would write of her upcoming stay in the jungle: bare minimum life, survival, et al. Contrarily, I knew that all she would have to go through would be bad food. Another said he would write of his experience on an island, a journey he was about to undertake. Interestingly, everyone talked about finishing the assignment before these little endeavors, so that they could "enjoy happily" without the sword of it hanging over their heads. You know how these things weigh us down. When I sourly explained all this over dinner, my parents said they would try to plan "one such trip" before the end of summer.

The first few days at the estate, I spent time loitering around the plantation as the men brought in new patios and beds for spreading the cherries and beans in batches. I sat with them, at times, hoping to pick up on something as some of the women shared their innocent thoughts and asked questions about the city and the ways of people like me. Only, their eyes lit up with unadulterated awe and impossible aspirations. And when my father gave an unhindered look of burning me up for wasting the laborers' time, whom he had hired by the hour, I decided to shut down my options of finding anything relevant on the field. Besides, it was getting unreasonably hot. And in the lonely village where people were minding their businesses over their suppressed but abdicated fears and plainly straightforward desires, I was the only one looking actively for a lead or lesson. In this medieval oil press, it seemed like I was the only one meddling with its steam and decanting an adulterant into its perfectly running system.

The next day, I adorned the small table in the cabin, which was to be our home for the summer, with my pile of books with illustrious covers and laptop and decided to do some reading. A fine summer judgment, I told myself, even as my hopes dwindled underneath the garb. By afternoon, I realized that the cabin wasn't a consolation either, for the heat struck the roof like a billion swords. The room had pale green, plastered but mounded walls and a rustic red-oxide flooring—a kind of motley which was under the threat of getting extinct. Despite the fan running its rotations in its entirety, the air it blew was hot. And just by sitting on the chair, my mul cotton shirt was drenched in my own sweat. It felt very muggy. As soon as I realized that detaching my damp back from the chair brought forth this disclosure, I decided to stick my back against the chair and swayed back and forth on the hind legs of the chair as I pressed the spine of my book against the rim of the table.

The peepal tree right outside the only vast window of the cabin brought some dismayed, slow breeze. It was better than not having any at all. With it came the subtle silences and the intermittent monologues of melodies exuded by birds whose names I did not know. It was all splendid until a crow came into the scene and began to caw like never before. I could not decide what was more annoying, the heat or the intrepid cawing. So much so that I fell off my chair backward in the confusion. It was when I was dusting off my augmenting pain that I saw a giant lizard, the size of a small ruler scale, at 45 degrees on the nook of the pale-green wall by the side of the window.

I went back to my book for a while, or I tried, but the mere knowledge of the presence of this giant, ogre-like creature in the cabin had split my attention into two. He was dark and slimy, and its sight sent jitters down my body. I tried not to look again. But then I looked at it again. I hated it. I wouldn't root for its existence. An enemy. I shuddered to shake the feeling off my body. He seemed in the prime of his age, just like me. Maybe just experienced enough, as I was. Had seen just about enough of the world, as I had. Nonetheless, the point in the timeline of our lives was such that you have understood enough, but then again, you always fell short. It stood still, yet I could see its energy and agility to conquer a territory. Maybe he was hungry, the heat slowly taking away all his bodily reserves. Every time I went into my book, he would move a little. He knew there was a bigger, more domineering creature up the pecking order and quickly played possum as soon as I looked. Every time. Not even a tremble! This was our own game of *Trip to Jerusalem*, and it went on for a while, only he outwitted the music master throughout.

The cawing outside continued in intermittent imitations and continuous repetitions of notes and intonations, much to my annoyance. It was either a strange crow or had instilled strangely fused but brilliant cawing methods to mark territorial integrity. He made fantastic sounds of squirrels which hopped on dangerously to the branches and catenary wires of electricity. He cawed again for a while to reinforce his crow-hood and began imitating the little birds of the tree that flittered in and out of the branches and twigs.

I looked away again, and when I looked back at the wall, he had moved again and stopped and played possum yet again. I tried to get back to my book, but the entire vicinity was now compromised, just as my attention. I finally threw my book and dumped myself on the bed and succumbed to nothingness. I turned to it. I hated its dark, devilish skin even more and decided to do a small experiment. I slept face down for a couple of minutes, making my distraction obvious and expecting him to even go on a merry-ride all over the wall. Lo and behold, this time the bastard hadn't moved, as if he had been aware of my little experiment like a snoop with a foreboding premonition. Discouraged, I tried to think about the book again, but I was tempted to devour on this detestation that had become all-pervading. I must admit I did not expect this giant little thing to weave out such intricate intelligence and play a delicate little dangerous game with someone much bigger and a potential threat. But then, maybe he thought, life is too fleeting to not play a game.

As I lay there, measuring the movement of the light on the wall with my fingertips, I thought about the lizard's genetic make-up, its evolution, the heat in its body, the influence of the local climate. As the clock struck 2, the rays lazed and slowly drew a trajectory over what now had turned into an odd, distasteful green wall in contrast to an equally distasteful red-oxide flooring.

In my distracted state, I saw him move swiftly downward with a big electric jerk and great celerity. I cringed and alerted myself like an unarmed warrior at war, whose only weapons at disposal were senses and stimuli. The enemy had made a sudden uninformed notorious move and positioned himself at a vantage point. He had seen something. But what? *Must be a prey*, I thought quite logically, *perhaps a bug*. It took me several minutes to figure out a camouflaged grasshopper lying mellow on a twig in between a bunch of leaves of the peepal tree whose crown had trespassed through the cabin window. I looked more closely from where I was. The grasshopper was just a bit more than a baby. But not so young to not know the business of being preyed upon and being caught as prey. For a while nothing happened. The lizard looked perplexed, still waiting for the right time, studying the situation and waiting cautiously like a tiger; while the cricket looked gaiety, still under the impression that its camouflage was working. The grasshopper's brown antenna twitched, in an attempt to test the tenacity of its nimrod: *was he worth the fight?* The twitch set the lizard again in swift motion, and it moved another inch or two closer like a man realigning against an approaching fast train. The grasshopper was now certain that the camouflage was long gone. Alerted, for several minutes, the cricket showed absolutely no sign of life, so much so that my vision began to wander away and I had to strenuously search to fix my spot on it again. When you look at the second hand for a long time, the certainty of the ticks becomes so great that your eyes deceive, and you see or you allude that it has exhibited one backward tick. Such was the deception that there was even a moment when I thought what happened had been my imagination and that the grasshopper had merely been a toy insect or a twig.

For the grasshopper, strategically, the exit option was quite simple. To simply spread its wings and hop or fly onto the neighboring twig that ran parallel to the one it was on. This savior twig was right outside the window, which meant a leap would make it practically inaccessible to the wall-mounted lizard. He twerked his head in that direction and it almost did look like he was about to… But wait. No. He, too, wanted to play the game. It came so naturally to him, nothing else could be as involuntary. He knew that if he were to take the escape route, the moment he would turn his back and lose focus from the situation, his hunter would seize the chance. Moreover, the lizard was dangerously close and, with a quick pounce and a slick lick, he knew he would be dead meat. And he was not a small bug or a worm to be easily preyed upon. A brave front.

Yet again, the crow continued, only through voice, the voice of a lachrymose, afternoon boredom. When the sun is shining too bright to be bored. I wanted to get a glimpse of it, to show my intolerance to its feeling of being an unsung being. If only he could see through my eyes the hackneyed, displeasing caws he was sending out, he would see for himself how unruly it all was at the moment in a world where two other creatures were dangerously living on the edge. At least one of them was.

On the wall, a pause came again and lasted several minutes, each not taking any further action. I forgot all about the book and was invested in the bearings this battle was about to bring. The devilish lizard did not seem so devilish anymore. He was only looking for a mid-day meal. In that moment, a comfort set in, and my mind was focused singularly on the nature of things. The ingrained decision-making, the primal motivation driven through millions of years. The rawness of the wild contrasted with how humankind was living in a bubble built by himself, creating complex derivatives of this basic animal instinct. An elementary, billion years of earthen choices extrapolated into a multi-million industry of absurdity. Neither of these two had any parasol of protection over their exposed bodies. Everything was bare, raw, and exposed. There was no room for manipulations or any acknowledgment of algorithms.

A sudden bang of the door shook me, but they were unperturbed. On the other side, there was more call for territorial integrity as the crow began cawing more viciously at a squirrel and a pair of sparrows that sprung around the branch playfully. This caused a lot of distraction and took away the stability of the branch as the squirrel hopped and jumped to the mid-level branches before disappearing even as the crow continued to caw for attention. That was a last chance, had the grasshopper been pruned in its skills. But then again, it probably knew that a lizard never hesitates to risk death to get a healthy meal. The mighty lizard probably wondered if he hadn't scared the grasshopper enough or if his mind was mangled in his final moments of languorous silliness like that of a rat savoring a poisoned cheese of death. For, the grasshopper was filled with gaiety in the eyes of adversity. But the lizard knew better, with each movement measured, he slowly advanced with a small step. Perhaps, it was a moment the grasshopper was thinking of home, of its mother, and wished immediately to be unseen, to disappear. The gaiety had come, crashing. Outside the crow cawed away, this time mimicking the creatures in the domain.

What came next was a pure decantation of an ingrained behavior, which unfolded like an unaccustomed, newborn infant. I couldn't tell for sure, but there was a motion for appeasement by the grasshopper, with dilated eyes, that happens right before death strikes. Just as the wick of the candle burns brighter and higher before extinguishing, the senile crow sent out high-pitched caws and harsh cries mixed with strenuous imitations of a chimeric creature. The air filled with spookiness bearing a portent misfortune, the kind that hovered over the skies of the kingdoms facing imminent war and death. The warp and weft that had woven out an unhinged freedom of volition was about to disintegrate.

Both were on the same wall, inhaling the same puffs of air, relishing the same cool wind that now blew from the peepal tree onto each other's bodies, the same rays touching their skins and exoskeletons and suffering the same equilibrium and waging the same fight for survival. The lizard gravitated rapidly towards the twig. I wondered if the lizard had any shame. For having sidelined me and overlooking my presence. For having moved past me and bringing ignominy to my own eyes. He had long forgotten that the game began between me and him. For having taken my humungous existence for granted, rendering me lethargic and irrelevant in this game of life. Any harm from me was an idea too far-fetched. I collected myself for it was easy to slip into a state of dementia at these thoughts of primal predispositions. As the lizard had finished savoring the grasshopper, something swooshed out of nowhere, and before I knew it, all were gone. When I looked outside, I saw an eagle relishing its prey. Only the distasteful pale-green wall remained against which hung an assortment of green leaves. And in that spot where I first located the lizard, an act of instinct lingered. This archetype sent ripples that settled in my mind like a piece of moiré. And I didn't worry about my assignment anymore.

SUMMER BRUNT BROUGHT BY A BONFIRE

Someone asked me what was the worst thing I had done in my life. It sent me into a tizzy. My gut twitched. I quickly collected myself, but the story ran in my head.

I was about fifteen in '92 when we moved to K-colony. It was my father's second posting at the hydroelectric plant. He was a geologist. And before the end of that year, I had gained notoriety for being a bully – both in school and the neighborhood. I looked through people, learned their vulnerabilities, and hit them where it hurt them the most. My age and the times were such that vulnerabilities were unfiltered and profound. Vulnerabilities were too evident. And no one had mastered the art of concealment. Too short, too tall, too dark-skinned, too fair-skinned, crooked adolescent teeth, left-handed, I targeted them all. Medium skin? Wheaty? I called them all out. Schadenfreude.

My father was the exact opposite of me – a middle-aged pushover living timidly under the aegis of his father who had brought himself down "dutifully" to the K-colony. On the other hand, my grandfather was a bully just as I. And my father lived like a suppressed colonial under his father's dictatorial spell. Recessive traits skip a generation. Now I know. Refusing to treat his adult son as an adult, my grandfather exuded power and control. It even took the form of loud admonishments, leaving it no secret in the neighborhood. To keep myself ahead of this dome of humiliation that rested on my household, to feed my esteem, to requite the lost power, I bullied. I relished mass power and savored the fear in the eyes of the succumbed. The more the bully fed my ego, the more I beefed him up. By the end of the year, I was this ball of fleshy, big-mouthed monstrosity. *Now* I know.

The K-colony had well-defined asphalt roads that turned green each year under the spell of monsoons. Each road had several blocks, and each block had four houses called quarters. Everyone got along well – either had fun with friends, did potluck, salon evenings, gossip, games, or feuded with their mismatches. But everyone was in a convenient, familiar loop running the same blues. Always. Everyone except two families – the colony's doctor couple who had no kids and the Nadgirs, a family that had two sons. The doctor couple suffered the pain of childlessness by remaining private and nobody bothered them. The Nadgirs' older son was about my age and the younger one was about 7 or 8. Despite having children, the Nadgirs refused to be a part of the community. They never joined the potluck or the game of *Housie* that happened fortnightly or caught up on the evening gossip or partook in sports. In the evenings, after his sons went to bed, Mr. Nadgir drank by himself, sitting on the porch of his quarters, with a mellow classical music audible only to him. Mrs. Nadgir hardly came out. She was city-bred, unlike the other women of the colony. Her rich parents stayed in the city, and so did all of her sisters. The women of the colony, in her view, had sheepishly followed the men they had been married to. But not her. Mr. Nadgir had been married into her household after her father had obtained some promises from him. So, she always believed she was a notch above the other women. She wore the choicest of sarees and had the softest of silks draped around her at all times. Initially, some of the women tried to humor her, but after repeated cold-shouldering, they gave up. And the hush-talk about her being a snub began. None of the other blocks had any kind of fencing, but a bamboo fence built around the Nadgirs' garden mocked what lay on the other side, marking a lackluster boundary where sometimes the boys played with each other. Very rarely, Mrs. Nadgir allowed them to play with other children but only when the other children played in the common area of their block. The lack of peers made them quite timid, and they stammered when they tried to speak to others. Such factors soon made them a pariah and alienated them further.

As for me, the dimensions and expanse of my bullying manifested into a revelry when around them. The specifics were myriad. Oh, where to start the act! Taunts rejoiced in the air around my head when I saw them. I went crazy! And limitless! I even vilified their family name using undertones and my skilled connotations. It became an opprobrium to be associated with that surname all over the colony. Any game played with them was a sham, and the "real" game began once they left. They continued to remain timid and hung on their face a look of constant sullen temperance and an occasional confusion showed itself as a visage of calmness akin to a deer. But not once did they fight against me when I made fun of them in front of everyone. Timid.

When you bully, it is always about you, it's never about them. It stayed that way with the Nadgirs, up until the incident of basket. Up until then, the Nadgir family or its existence made no difference to me. There was nothing much to be done in a colony like that – no theaters, no restaurants, no public parks or play areas. A lot of time, no opportunities. So, people talked. But let me be clear about my parents. They were mere onlookers and passive listeners to the great afflictions the Nadgirs were, and never once were they a part of the propaganda that ran against them.

One evening, Mother had asked me to come to the vegetable vendor's stall as soon as I was done playing. When I got there, Mother was already there, picking up leafy vegetables from the bottom lot of the basket. She always claimed that they put the fresher ones at the bottom. "They want to exhaust the oldest lot first."

Mrs. Nadgir came from the other side of the road and stood there like she was not meant to be there at that gloaming hour, not doing that thing she was about to do.

The bundle of shopping bags had almost wrung my mother's skin on the wrist. So, I took over the lot from her and stood leaning on the green pillar by the side of the stall as she moved on to the basket of tomatoes. Mother lost her balance a bit and moved backward, knocking off Mrs. Nadgir's little sequin purse. "Oh, sorry about that," she said with a warm evening smile and immediately picked up the purse, dusting it off. "I felt a mild blaze." Mrs. Nadgir was as stuck-up as she always was. As Mother moved on to the citrons, her eyes vacillated between the citrons and the twine basket that Mrs. Nadgir held in her other hand.

The maker had wrapped and wreathed the basket like a vine entwined around the trunk of a tree. He had left just enough interstices and yet managed to beautifully articulate the air into it in order to help the container breathe. The choice and placement of bristles protected it from any exposure to unexpected rain or dust. But, to be honest, I thought the handles had been too stiff and much farther apart to be held in a fist. Its luxury and vogue compromised comfort. It was nothing extraordinary or unaffordable, but its mere possession instilled an ease. A comfort of sorts. Mother was not the kind to be greedy but had a good eye for things that once invested proved durable.

"Nice basket! Where did you get it?" she finally remarked, as I took a step back and stood leaning on another dirty-green, worn-out wooden pillar, waiting.

"Oh! These things have a way of finding me! My servant in Dharwad got it from the flea market!" She was unimpressed with its beauty and began to pick her vegetables in a disorderly fashion.

"Where is this market? My husband has a court appearance over the issue of land rehabilitation in the coming week. Maybe I can ask him to get a similar one," Mother got chatty and persisted.

Mrs. Nadgir, with a smirk, said, "Sorry, dear! I don't really know. Besides, it's not for everyone. Don't bother. It's quite expensive, and I am sure it's not in your taste."

That was it. Mother paid the vendor, turned her back and left. She grabbed back all the bags from me, clenched her fists so hard around them, and did not utter a word the entire way back. Later that night in bed, she recounted it all to my father in the darkness, assuming I was fast asleep. But I heard it all, how she was left humiliated.

I threw a silent fit onto the pillow, and at that moment, the bully had crossed over the fencing and burned in the fire for revenge. A meaningless revenge, a silly revenge, a snub, a vilifying revenge. But a revenge nonetheless. More sarcasm and more atrocity followed at every possible opportunity and everywhere – on the school grounds, in the lunch hours, on their porch, on the untarred, muddy roads. I chased them, pushed them, roughed up against them at every chance. Until they stopped coming out for whatever little play they used to. But that didn't seem enough. I was still lurching like a lecher for a bang, for a more suitable opportunity to exact my revenge.

Then came summer. Proximity to the coastline made the season unbearably hot and humid. As soon as the examinations concluded, everyone retired to their hometowns for the holidays. Only a few families stayed put to hear the empty roads bellow in pain, awaiting the colony to beckon some life and laughter.

The Nadgirs were leaving too, just like everyone else. I remember the day vividly, as I stood with my back to their block and played catch with a nearly dead tennis ball, bouncing it off the high wall of the quarters. The parents came dragging their suitcases while the boys carried food and drinks for the journey in that twine basket. I turned around to bounce the ball off the cement floor, and my eyes met theirs. Neither did I greet them, nor did they acknowledge me. The boys' faces twitched in confidence as they knew I would not touch them when they were around their parents. The twine basket irked me as they disappeared around the corner of the street. Word was around that Mrs. Nadgir's mother was bedridden, and they were going to spend the entire summer in the city. I couldn't do much, other than bumping a punch against my palm in disappointment.

I spent the initial days loitering around the roads, stopping by to catch up or play a silly game with those who stayed back. Soon, some of us grew close and formed a small tentative group that hung around to play the same old meaningless games. We explored the untouched corners of the colony, trespassed the fencing of the algae-ridden sheds, broke a window or two to unearth some kind of mystery no one seemed to have noticed so that we could surprise everyone when they returned. All we found were some broken drainage pipes and unhinged electric poles. And when boredom set in by noon, we went home. I ranted about us not going to our hometown for the summer. And my protests were always drowned by the constant nagging of my grandfather.

The coming of Holi brought some action, and we began making elaborate plans to resurrect a *Holika*. We said it was going to be bigger than ever and that we would burn all the boredom with it. Everyone was assigned a specific task. One group was in charge of bringing old, ragged clothes. Another group was to go to the fringes of the forest to collect some dried and fallen twigs and possibly some logs. I was to make the effigy of *Holika* grand. Mother took pity and said she'd arrange some flowers, crops, jaggery, coconut, and such things meant for the ritual of the pyre. The unused parking area beside our porch was designated as the place of the bonfire. It made an ideal spot as it was mostly worn-out cement flooring and did not have any trees or homes in its vicinity. By noon, everyone piled up their findings in the corner of the cleared parking lot and prayed there would be no unseasonal rains.

As for me, the joy of playing with *gulal* had ended as soon as I had crossed over to adolescence. I now only smeared the younger ones with their own bundle of colors when they came popping around like translucent bubbles. That morning, I left a few of them teary-eyed when some of the colors hit their tastebuds during the roughing. They didn't find it merry anymore and ran to their mothers. Amidst all this, there had been a slip-up. I had missed buying the *gulal* required for the ritual, which Mother insisted was mandatory. So after lunch, I decided to go and buy some.

It was late afternoon, but the sun was still strong. So, on my way back, I had to stop to catch a breath right in front of the deserted quarters of the Nadgirs. My eyes lit up. I wiped off my sweat beads and sat on the small culvert to give it a thought. A tarnish here? Some smear there? Fill the water tank with colors? Ideas popped in my head like lined-up notes in music. Almost immediately, I heard rustles from a tarpaulin sheet from behind the culvert. There was a small muddy, pebbly path that led to the backyard of the Nadgirs. Now, every one of us had played in every other person's backyard over the last year, except the Nadgirs'. Never the Nadgirs'. So, I simply got curious and took that pebbly path. Who was to stop me! I saw a blue tarpaulin sheet sloped on either side of a rope held by two poles forming a tent. Right in front of the backyard door were a series of steps that led into a familiar cemented pit. All the houses had such pits for utility purposes. Beyond it was a well-maintained vegetable garden. A bat flew out of nowhere right into my face, and it was then that I saw some clothes on the clothesline – a pair of brown-black trousers and a blue-gray checkered shirt which had dried up beyond necessity, leaving it half-faded. *Mr. Nadgir must have hung it up before leaving,* I thought. I tried but not once could I imagine Mrs. Nadgir to have done such a chore. At the end of the clothesline was a turquoise satin handkerchief with a beautiful N engraved in red. It fluttered to the gushes of wind, struggling to escape the clutches of the clothespin that grounded it to the wire. The devil snapped in me, and I immediately pulled out the pants, the shirt, and the handkerchief with the N on it. I dashed over the vegetable garden, knocking off a pot or two on the way. I ran to the parking lot, hid the clothes amidst the ragged bundle and made sure it was well-concealed. It was a small win, and I rejoiced.

After sunset, everyone gathered near the porch in anticipation of the bonfire. Mother brought the coffee table from our verandah and placed all the trays containing the ritualistic materials at the nearest wall so that the children didn't topple it in their zest. Everyone had to bring their own chairs. They did so. All the ladies sat a little farther from the pile which now formed a mountain of logs, wood, clothes and other items. I could see the red 'N' partly jutting out over a piece of stick. I panicked, *what if someone noticed!* What if the elders asked who the beautiful piece of satin belonged to and what it was doing in the bonfire? I looked around, looked into everyone's eyes to see if anyone was interested in it. But each was occupied with their own matters. The ladies chattered away, some ran behind their toddlers, who seemed to be intrigued by this huge mountain in front of them. The men didn't bring any chairs, as they preferred to stand in groups and discuss work. So, they watched from afar. Some children ran around the huge pile, brushing their hands against the heap. I had to chase them off.

It was a clear night sky, and the stars twinkled above. I tried not to think that people knew. It was only when the pyre was lit that I heaved a sigh of relief, found a bit of solace, and enjoyed the evening. We threw in the crops, the colors, and danced around the bonfire, celebrating the destruction of *Holika.* The effigy came crumbling down, and I could see the 'N' rise up in the embers. A meager vengeance or so I thought. I soon forgot about the whole thing. It was not unnatural or unexpected for people to steal clothes during *Holika dahan*. It was only that it was I who stole it from the Nadgirs' house, and I knew that if anyone learned of it, they would think that I did it out of spite. If you are thinking this was the worst thing that I did, no. I would have moved on if that was the end. The Nadgirs would return home with a pair of clothes short. Not a big deal.

In the last week of summer, the people of the colony began to return slowly before the next term began. But that day, the roads were still deserted as usual, and the clouds loomed over the sky, foreboding the monsoons. The Nadgirs got down at the bus station and walked on that desolate road towards their home. Only, this time there were only three of them. Mrs. Nadgir was clad in a simple white saree, which was unusual, and no ornaments adorned her. The boys walked beside her, their heads hung like flamingos, with a ghostlike pallor on their faces. Soon, men and women gathered near their house. I went, too, surrounded by some friends. Mrs. Nadgir stood right outside their porch, staring at the house differently, tears rolling down her cheek. The women began to console her, as they slowly walked her inside. Only the older son spoke.

"Papa was getting medicines for *Ajji*, and while he was crossing the road, he was hit by a truck."

Everyone gasped in disbelief and looked at each other's faces in search of some kind of explanation.

"When did this happen?" one of the men asked.

"About a month ago. On the day of Holi."

My heart skipped a beat. A thrust bolted from the pit of my gut and hung on the deep wall of my throat, thronging my mouth, seeping it with fearful saliva from all sides. The probing went ahead and more details came of the incident when suddenly Mrs. Nadgir got up from the sofa and began to look hysterically for something.

"Where is it? Where is it?" she mumbled in her frenzy.

"What is she looking for?" the women asked, still in disbelief, not knowing if they had to let her be or console her. "Let her rest. We will help her find anything she wants," they offered.

The boys kept mum even as their mother unfolded everything in the house. A neighbor got some milk, juices and snacks. Two of the women sat the boys down on the sofa. They drank a glass of milk and, with tears in their eyes and sobs stuck in words, they recited the anecdote which they seemed to have heard a million times now. "On their last anniversary, Mother had bought a satin handkerchief and had it engraved with an 'N' on it. On one of their evening walks, a friend talked about how beautiful her handkerchief was. While mother had said she had liked its color, father had taken to humor and said, 'She's bought it to wipe her tears with it when once I die!' and burst into a hearty laugh. She's looking for it."

My diabolical heart swarmed with a deluge of disgust. My head reeled and a sudden ache ranted words of dismal consternation like a pack of night dogs howling into nothing.

A truck pulled up in front of the block and soon began to pack and load things. The people of the community did everything they could to help the Nadgirs finish and conclude.

So, when someone recently asked me the worst thing I had done in my life, it sent me into that tizzy I had felt in my gut back in that moment. The moment I realized I had done the worst thing. The question had limped around the table on my drunk dinner companions. All of them doctors. One said he had overdosed a patient with 70 percent burns and caused his death. The next one said he once left a tiny bundle of synthetic suture in the patient's organ while stitching the surgical incision, and they had to do it all over again. Another doctor recalled the incident that happened while working at the government hospital – she had triaged a patient assuming there was time for the lady to dilate. Before she realized, the baby was crowning, and as soon as she rushed the woman to the delivery room and placed her in position, the baby fell down into the bucket meant for amniotic fluid and placenta. Everyone at the table cringed. These were all accidental and discretions that had turned disastrous. Mine was not. So, I eluded the question.

The Man Who Didn't Leave

We were all sitting in the bosom of the big banyan tree, surrounding ourselves with its cool, calculated breeze. Its roots hung overhead like little rattlesnakes. The big banyan tree overlooked the state highway and was situated on the other side of it. Children ran around the labyrinthine adventitious roots that had, over the years, reached the ground to provide support to the big tree. In front of us was the lake, with the high sun glimmering on its surface. At three o'clock, a bunch of bare-bodied, sun-roasted yet accustomed children sat, pelting stones into an already perturbed lake.

Amidst the enormous 200-year-old banyan tree and its maze was a small and simple temple, just enough to hold a sculpted godly stone and a lighted lamp which was always strewn about with fresh and writhed marigolds. Nobody could enter it except the priest who, only by the extension of his arm, bathed the sacred stone nestled inside and offered the daily offerings to the deity, the village goddess. Today, the priest sat readying all the things for the cremation – of Sasikumar; his junior next to him was building a stretcher with slit bamboo extensions.

All the village heads and prominent members of the community sat in mourning under the cool shade of the banyan tree. After morosely discussing the harvest, the appointment of the post-master general and the funds for the government school, one of them declared, "Sasi never wanted to go," addressing the elephant in the room.

Others were only too keen to take it further.

"No, he did not."

"He wanted anything, but to leave his land."

"Even now, when I think of him, the first thing that comes to my mind is that he did not want to go."

"The only other thing that comes to *my* mind are his bald head and bushy eyebrows. But yes, he did not want to go; he would say that at least once a day."

"My land may be barren as the sand of the ocean..."

"...Till my last breath, this shall be my station," another completed his words.

One of them, a college boy, was doing and undoing a rollout of what looked like an application form.

"What's that?" an elderly man asked.

"Death certificate form."

"But his body is not here."

"Yes. But we still have to get it in the Local Civil Registrar."

A cool but eerie breeze blew, bringing with it the smell of a deathly smoke from a bodiless house. It was the first house in the old village. Anyone entering the village first met with the house of Srinathkumar, Sasikumar's father, who sat outside with his accounting books, occasionally looking up across his gold-rimmed glasses. Next was Sundaramma's house; she was Srinathkumar's sister. Sundaramma was a widow and had lived with her daughter Renu, until she married her off to a man who lived in the West.

"Where exactly was it?"

"Who knows! Some godforsaken country! They are all the same."

"But Renu was the only one Sasi ever loved."

"Moreover, after she left him to marry an NRI, he emphasized much further that he would not leave."

"Do you all remember when he was called by some foreign government to present his methods in their university? He refused outright. They had even offered him monetary rewards."

"Tch! He was from a different league. This village was too small for his caliber. After all even our government awarded him for his innovative farming methods."

"Sundaramma didn't do justice to Sasi and Renu. As soon as the priest got the proposal of that '"NRI"' man, she jumped and pushed for the wedding."

"Pft! Some NRI! Phanindra said he was a janitor in some school there! Renu and Sundaramma only found out later, much after the wedding."

"I wonder what changed Sasi's heart! That he went to meet her again. Otherwise, he probably would be alive today!"

"Maybe that's why our elders said not to ever run behind, woman, gold, or land. It will leave you in ruins."

"When she married and left to the West, he became a different person; it was as if he had created a bubble around himself. A bubble that only had this land of ours, this old village, and deity." Everyone turned to the deity with folded hands. "And anything outside the bubble meant her and her presence."

"But he was happy, never fretted over her!"

"Never."

"When she told him she was marrying someone else, neither did he question her, nor did he try to persuade her. 'Should I beg?' were his words."

"Renu! That wretched woman! He should never have met her again! She had become more conniving than Sundaramma was, and used him to her advantage. Sasi failed to see that."

"It was not in her fate to lead a noble life!"

"Maybe that was why God did not bless her with a child."

"So many years, since all of it. He was the noblest of men not only in our village but in the entire colony." He joins his hands in the direction of the house and mutters some prayers. "We can only aspire to be like him. What could we do? We cannot advise against the will of a grown man and his decision, can we?"

"All of us thought about it in our hearts, but none uttered a word to him."

"How could we have interfered or advised, good or bad?"

"Especially not to a man of his stature."

The boy with the application form rolls it into a cylindrical tube and runs his excuse for a small pen into it, bringing it out from the other side.

"Fill it up already!"

"Ah, yes, yes… Name – Sa-si-ku-mar. It reminds me of the story of this girl in my college – very religious, always wore two plaits, and looked like a pigtailed little school girl. And she always covered herself completely! From head to toe! Either a half saree or a salwar kameez, full arms! And when those outgoing girls wanted to be 'modern', she flinched at the choices of these girls, cringing her face at their body-fitting clothes or crop tops," the young man narrated.

"Ah, I know what happened in the end. Didn't they all beat her up? The girls?" another boy said.

"That was only a consequence. The finale was the most brutal. I mean, not for us, but upon her. On the day of the fest, in front of an audience, her entire ensemble for the play came down, and she was left half naked amidst roars of reverberating laughter at the irony in front of them."

"She ran away and never returned to the college again."

"Poor girl."

"Age – 58, Father's name – Srinathkumar," he continued to write trying to hold back the impressionable corners of the paper.

"These things, these words, and thoughts have a way of working into our lives," one of the elderly said.

"We are treading on a path left by our thoughts. The mind thinks first and then it happens. *Occurs*."

"So true. And it occurs just as we think it is or in its antithetical manifest. To say 'you were wrong' or 'you thought too much about it'."

"But Sasikumara was a man of honor. He did not want to leave because he was fond of his land, his country."

"He was like this banyan tree. Spread over everyone."

"Mother's name – What was his mother's name?"

"Vanamala."

"Mother's name – Vanamala. Marital status – unmarried. Children – None."

"Why did that wretched woman come back into his life? After that, he changed."

"At this age! After all these years!"

"Phanindra said her husband used to beat her up. And also, her daughter."

"Daughter?"

"The adopted one. And one day in his drunken state he attempted to violate her honor. So, she grabbed her daughter and ran away from him. At least that's what Renu says happened. She didn't know who to turn to for help. Sasikumara learned of the situation from Phanindra and the noble man that he was, he assured her of helping her and her daughter. A sobbing woman is like a drug on the man's brain. She played the trick of helplessness."

"Maybe he had loved her all his life, even while she was away."

"Yes. He didn't marry anyone."

"But he had turned a bit rowdy, coming across as a bloody man. But deep inside he always had a mother's heart."

Everyone nodded in agreement. A stream of violent ripples splashed on the shore of the lake, as children began to throw heavier and heavier stones into the water.

"She was a serpent in the form of a woman!"

"How did he die?" asked the young man.

"Such stories are not for younglings like you."

The young man left to get some other documents from Sasikumar's house. The others continued.

"Last month, one afternoon, Sasi came to Rangaiah's house and asked for some money. Maybe to help her, or set up a house or for a lawyer, nobody knows. Each one had his own opinion of why he asked for such a hefty amount. He would never reveal anything on that day. Not even to Rangaiah."

"But everyone knew of the situation and he began to grow impatient. Rangaiah swears he heard him rant and even said *what a waste of life!*"

"It was when he began to process his tickets that everyone understood. As to who was in that faraway and forbidden country and why he wanted *that* money."

"He would do anything for Renu, even back then, before she dumped him and his feelings like garbage."

"And then, he went away, in the middle of the night. Not a word to anyone! When Phanindra said he had received him there…"

"Yes, yes. The call," a couple of them said in unison.

"Then everything was confirmed," everyone said in chorus.

A thick, heavy smoke rose from the earthen pot further behind them, as if to make up for the absence of a dead body.

"How are they going to ensure this ritual without his body?"

"Someone said they are getting his ashes?"

"You can't put something on a pyre that's already burned."

"Does his sister know of his death?"

"How does it matter now? They estranged over the death of their parents and swore never to set foot in each other's houses."

"Their parents' burial was more tragic."

"Was it worse than not having a dead body in front of one's own house?"

"It's a curse on the family"

"It was the only time he came close to leaving the colony."

"It's so strange, the son was close to his father and the daughter was close to the mother."

"Isn't it that woman who hid her ailment because she wanted to die before her husband?"

"Vanamala."

"She did not want to undergo any treatment. Hospitals terrified her."

"What a stupid woman!"

"Pray, what a gutsy woman! To be going through the end of days all alone."

"Anyway, when Vanamala knew her days were nearing, she insisted on going to her daughter. And upon reaching there, spoke of strange things to the grandchildren, like love and forgiveness, things that fill a person on the deathbed. The daughter, unsuspecting, went to work. And her mother had collapsed by the time she had returned."

"Because of the high costs of treatment, she immediately sent her mother back for further treatment."

"She couldn't fly back with her, said she had work commitments; but promised to follow in a couple of days."

"Yes, she didn't come with her."

"And before the daughter could come here, she had passed away. Ugh! And the pus in her body! They said they removed buckets of pus! It was so bad they couldn't keep the body for a long time. So, they buried her before the daughter could see her for one last time."

"Sasikumar ensured everything went smoothly. Srinath was in a state of shock."

"Yes, even after this, the brother and sister were in a reasonably good relationship."

"It was the father's death that changed things."

"About 5 years had passed since Vanamala's death. Srinath was in good health when he went to visit his daughter. At his niece's wedding a few days before, he too spoke like a person nearing death."

"He called Sasikumar aside, and with tears rolling down his eyes, he spoke about the familial misfortunes of his son. The father lamented that he would have to die leaving his son alone in this world."

"And then he flew."

"And then he flew. To his daughter. Within a week news came that he had died of a heart attack. Instantly. The daughter tried her best to preserve the body in the facility for some time, till her brother could go to see his father's face for one last time."

"That was the first time Sasikumar actually pondered about leaving the village and even the country."

"Yes. Visa and processing took a lot of time and the cost of keeping the body of their father in the facility became too much for her. She cremated their father in that faraway land. Sasikumara was furious and called his sister names and cursed her for doing so."

"He begged her to send the body back. But she did not."

"Some said she did it to take revenge. Because Sasi had not waited for her during their mother's burial. She had held her mother dear to her heart."

"She said she would never set foot into the colony again. They went separate ways after that."

"They did," everyone said in unison. The children began to pick up large pieces of bricks and began to splash into the water.

"Hey!! Get out of here!" one of the older men screamed. The priest's assistant had almost completed making the bamboo stretcher now. And there was a long, uneasy pause. Without a body, there was nothing left to do but ponder over death itself.

"It's a curse on the family. Every married couple immediately after the marriage must come and offer coconut, ghee, honey, milk, and fruits, and light a lamp to the goddess. But Srinath and Vanamala did not. They said it's all superstitions. The sin committed comes back and the generations carry it forward. Only to suffer. See, Sasikumar did not even get married. It's all the karma of his parents."

"Yes, there is no other plausible explanation. Was he not handsome? Was he not wealthy? Was he not honorable? He was every bit the most eligible man in the colony."

"Karma always plays its bit. Despite repeated requests, many of them followed them. They said they were the first to get educated, they had seen the world. That they know…"

The young man returned, "I will hand over these documents in the office; they are yet to attach an approval letter."

"I hope she gives him a worthy burial there."

ORDER OF THINGS

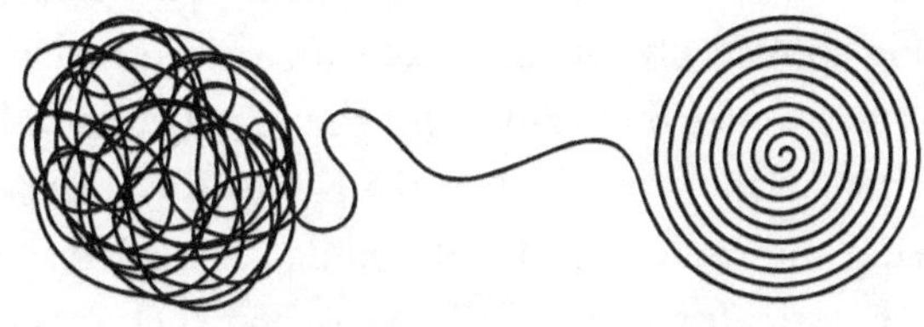

In the three months that Mani had worked at the big house that belonged to Srinathkumar, a former *Jahagirdar*, he had never disobeyed an order. Srinath was not a *Jahagirdar* anymore. He now held a place of power in the to-be colony's administration, but everyone still referred to him as the *Jahagirdar* simply because of his lineage.

Vanamala, the wife of the *Jahagirdar*, the lady *Jahagirdar*, sat behind the metal grill that had been raised as a buffer to separate the inside from the outside and hurled out instructions, commands, plain abuses, and ways of work over Mani. Never appreciation. For her, of utmost importance was the order of the work. At first, Mani had been hired mostly to pluck jasmines from the vine that had grown far and wide. There was a sanctity attached to this act, an act of reverence, as it was well known in the entire village that the Jahagirdar himself took care of the vine and plucked its buds every evening for his evening prayers. That was until he got too old for it. Pulling out a ladder, climbing up, and targeting the buds using a longish, bent metal wire seemed like a risky task.

It was then that Mani had been hired, and he had been so glad to do this job! Mani was a larky man in his forties, whose cheeks had dissolved under his skin. He was marked by his white vest and dhoti and his grayish stubble. He had tousled hair that covered half of his face most of the time. He spoke only when spoken to, with a melancholy and dismissiveness that came with the many years of labor. Soon after, Mani was asked to work on other things too, like fixing the roof, cleaning the tank, clearing the drain, spraying pesticides, putting a rat trap, and such petty jobs. Every day there'd be a new job, unsaid or unheard of before. Such was the vastness of the garden. But mainly most of the work was taking care of the plants and bringing the harvests to fruition. Mani didn't mind working on anything as long as he got to pluck the jasmine buds that shone in the evening light like a thousand pearls. Despite the wife of the *Jahagirdar* giving him a hard time, he obeyed all the instructions. But, he wanted to pluck the jasmines after all the other works were completed. Somehow, Vanamala sensed that over the days, and she made sure he did not get to pluck it in the end by always giving more work after the jasmines or asking him to do that first as soon as he arrived. But Mani was desperate and decided to defy her orders.

That evening, Mani dusted off the tobacco dust gathered in the crevices of his clothes from working at the tobacco factory, his day job. The meager white vest and his long-forgone dhoti shivered like little kittens. The courtyard of the house, although big, was always gloomy and had a dark, algae-infested water tank in one corner. Vanamala always thought Mani's work was a sinecure for the pay her husband was handing out and always found something for him to do. That evening she decided to have him clean the water tank.

"It was last cleaned during Holi," she said, "when some rascals strew the tank water with colors. Clear the fronds of the coconut tree, one fell down today. But first, pluck the jasmines," she said as usual from behind the metal grill. Mani could hear her anklets as she walked to the inner quarters of the house.

Mani got some bleaching agents, giant brushes to clean the inner walls, and set to work. The bigger task was to get the tank emptied first. He grunted as he exerted his energy to unplug two sturdy pieces of cloth that had been pinched inside the small outlet hole. Muddy water gushed out slowly, elegantly as he turned to rake up the big chunks of dirt. When the water levels were knee-deep, he climbed its wall and jumped inside. The more he cleared, the more the outlet gushed out water in timed intervals.

"*Jahagirdar* will come for prayers. I told you to pluck the jasmines first, Mani," Lady *Jahagirdar* called out from behind the metal grill arriving again from the inner quarters of the house. Mani did not pay heed and continued to dredge and weed and dredge again. He threw out all the waste, and it filled the air with a mild stink. He removed his vest as if to deprive it of any more odor. He hung it on a nearby stone for a quick dry. His face was stern with inaction, which was very unlike him.

"The jasmines are for prayers. I told you to pluck it first before you dirtied and desecrated yourself with the muck from the tank."

Although Mani's face indicated a slight pretentious remorse, he knew he was going to pluck the buds only after he finished all the other work today. He, however, hastened the dredging and then quickly bleached the inner walls and floor of the tank, flushed it all out with water through the same outlet, and then plugged the outlet back with the same two ragged pieces of cloth. He kept the tap running so that the tank would fill up again.

No sooner did Mani arrive in the evenings, Vanamala called out with brazen authority, "*Jahagirdar* will be here for the jasmines." When in fact, not one day had the Jahagirdar arrived just until before the sun actually began to sink into the horizon. She was very well aware of it and yet she would infuse a sense of urgency, a sense of bearing over Mani. So much so that meaningful words had turned into a rhetoric. The tap had no washer and made blurting sounds maniacally, like they were taking away all the water that belonged to the village.

"Jasmines have not been plucked! And now the profanity! Dear Lord!" her chair creaked from the inside as she roared in anger. Mani seemed anxious but was unperturbed. He took on the next job and stepped aside to clear all the dried fronds and seeds from the two coconut trees that had piled up at the steps of the cloister. There were two coconut trees that stood like epitomes of insignificance. A long silence filled the air, marked by occasional rustles of the coconut fronds.

In all that time, over the span of 3 months, not once had Vanamala stepped out of that metal grill. So, Mani always imagined, her fuming by now, – a highly woman, clad in all-silk run with temple motifs, a big nose ring adorning her flaring nostrils, her hair filled with the jasmines from her garden strewn together, hands filled with bangles and a hefty necklace she wore around her neck, that sheltered her raspy voice.

He did not hear anything for a long time, until her arms kept two heirloom porcelain jars outside to the sun with a clinking thump and yelled, "Collect the lemons after you pluck the jasmines! I need to put pickles. But first the jasmines, Mani." Her voice was as brazen as it could get, and Mani knew he was now already in trouble with the *Jahagirdar*. He knew it from her voice that she would take it up. Mani didn't look up, lest it infest him with some kind of social burden. He knew she had stormed off because the rocking chair began to creak again.

Mani hesitantly picked up the lemon basket and walked towards the lemon shrubs like a thief guilty of his theft. His eyes teared up, which he quietly wiped off as he put on a solemn face. His heart thumped and was torn between guilty disobedience and his pressing, desperate needs. He wondered if he should just give it up and go back to just pluck the jasmines. But, it was too late for that now. He did not hear any creaking of the chair or any jingles of her. She had probably gone inside to bring the *Jahagirdar* or was just storming by herself in the *verandah*. Or simply refused to order anymore to this deviant servant. It would be beneath her to give the same instruction again and again and see it defied. He began to pick the lemons and divided them into groups of two. He then went to the sandpit and buried them in two separate corners, as he usually did, for the Lady *Jahagirdar* always prepared pickles in batches of 2.

"You think you know us too well. You are riding on us. You think I will not be able to find another person for this job?" her voice thundered from inside. "Just because the

Jahagirdar praised you a couple of times, you think we have gotten too accustomed to you to let you go?"

The water from the tap had now filled the tank, and it began to overflow thunderously.

"Sorry, *Amma*," was all Mani could blurt as his lifeless cheeks were soaked in tears.

"The *Jahagirdar* will hear about this. Consider this your last day," she thundered from inside.

Mani put on his dusty vest and let his dhoti reach its full length, the tobacco dust scooped up in the mild wind. He washed his hands and legs and picked up the silver basket from the pile of silverware kept for the evening prayers near the doorway. He looked up at the vast jasmine vine, as if for the last time. The buds had turned golden in the evening light. He forgot everything and smiled like a child. He washed his hands thoroughly, brushed his vest in the air, and put them on. All that he had done today – the disobeying, taking hurls of contempt, keeping his clothes as odor-free as possible, everything culminated to this point. He smelled his hands discreetly as he brought the bamboo ladder which the *Jahagirdar* had considered too heavy to lift now and hoisted it up against a stronghold of thick vines. He climbed up, carefully holding the silver basket in one hand and nipped the buds that were within his reach. He then climbed up another step and pulled out a rather long stick with a curved wire at its end, pulling the tendrils closer. Once they were within his reach, he nipped them. He suddenly realized that Vanamala had not spoken nor made any gestures for a long time. He was most certain that it would be his last day. When he got to the uppermost step of the ladder, he pulled the dancing tendrils closer, plucked the buds, and placed them in the basket. He got down and positioned the ladder to the next quarter and did the same. Like this, he covered the circumference of the vast vine.

When he was in the last quarter, he heard loud, affirmatively argumentative voices from inside the house. One was clearly of Vanamala and the other subtle, sober appeasing voice of the *Jahagirdar*.

The Jahagirdar would understand, Mani told himself. *He is a sensible man.*

The *Jahagirdar* came out slowly and asked in a calm voice, "What is this I hear, Mani? Is this why I hired you? To ruin the peace of the evenings?"

"It's because of your generosity that he is dancing on our heads today," Vanamala interrupted, "I am not being unreasonable. Last week I asked him to spray the pesticide and slice the guavas for the children. He didn't. And he keeps disrespecting my instructions."

The *Jahagirdar* turned to Mani to hear an explanation. Mani placed the silver basket on the table from where he had taken it and came and stood at a distance to the *Jahagirdar* with folded hands.

"*Anna*, I did spray the pesticide the following morning. It is winter and the early evening winds tend to spread it all over the garden and keep it in the air all night," Mani said in a hushed apologetic voice.

"You are not the master here. I am. You should know better to do as you are told," Vanamala was furious.

"Mani, once in a while is agreeable, but you cannot defy her orders every evening and do as you wish and how you wish. That *is* very disrespectful. And I know you are a man of stature."

Mani took a long pause, his head bent, and eyes gazing at his filthy feet and its badgered nails that didn't know a direction to grow into. "*Anna*, please forgive me. It's not that I cannot do what you ask of me or that I disobeyed intentionally. In the past year, I have given my wife a disease from working at the tobacco factory. She has fallen into a deathbed of which she is unaware. And each day I wish it had befallen me. She loves jasmines. Her face lights up. She loves how its fragrance takes the stinking smell of our bodies away. I used to buy her jasmines when I had money. Now I cannot afford any as I have spent everything I had on her treatment. When I pluck the jasmines at the end of the day, I am just hoping to catch as much fragrance as nature allows. The doctor says she is standing on death's door. But *Anna*, believe me, I have never tampered with the buds for selfish reasons. Every evening when I return, she grabs my palms and smells them. I could not take that away from her."

So saying, he turned to the gate and left, not using his palms lest they touch something. The wide vine stood tall in the receding evening light. Only one-quarter of it shone like pearls, and the rest of it was bereft of any flowers and descended into the darkness of the winter.

THE BEAUTIFUL LOCKED BRIDE

The children saw them first as they alighted from the bus. Even from a distance, they shone like newly sprung leaves of the Bakul tree—blithe in the air. As they approached, the children dropped their pebbles and marbles and ran to Bhaskara. Bhaskara's first wife had passed away, and after 3 months of grieving, he had descended on this lazy day with his new bride. The children grinned at them like evergreens and then looked down in shyness in the presence of this resplendent another-Bhaskara. They were seeing his new wife for the first time, but she could not be a stranger, not anymore, for she was an appendage of Bhaskara, who stood there trying to play the familiar game of a new husband. After a bit of dragging and pulling at Bhaskara's hands, they ran to tell their mothers, who were better accustomed to meeting the eyes of familiar strangers.

The women came in excitement, forgetting their own selves and the tasks at hand, but immediately realized that there was little familiarity about this new bride. And a shock—how much was it, three months? The children now went and grabbed the new bride's hands, the presence of their mothers having boosted their comfort and familiarity. They pulled her by her hands as she struggled to keep from tripping over their jaunty little feet. And the street instantly filled with the happiness of a house welcoming a newborn baby.

The circumstantial familiarity handed down by the bride began to be slowly rejected by the women in their minds. She was the fairest and the most beautiful. Her eyebrows cut against the skin like a blade of grass cutting the blue azure of the sky, and it carved out a shining triangular glabella between them. Her skin glowed with a creamy-milk texture in the misty morning sun, like the skin of every newlywed should. She had heavy, straight eyelashes that drooped like the pinnae of a coconut tree. Her heavy eyelids batted against the flesh of her cheeks, playing in merriment of shyness. And her eyes glanced everywhere in a joyous panic from all the attention. Her red tussar garment melted into her silk-like skin, and her golden bangles and choker held onto her in infatuation. Her hair was bundled into a bun, only slightly perturbed along the hairline by the arduous journey.

The initial enthusiasm of the women now subsided and they stepped back as if to exercise caution. They thought for a while and talked – *she couldn't be from around here.* Not in any of the surrounding villages had they seen such a woman who had such sharp features and a distinguished silhouette. The men soon gathered, with their eyes fixated on the wonderous woman, their mouths moved with questions prodding Bhaskara about the whereabouts of his new bride. It soon turned into a garrulous gaiety, a bit too much for men of their age. A fleeting glee ruptured through their bodies, in having witnessed something so rare – a feast to their eyes, an intrigue roused their barren hearts and a romance stirring their cynical lives. An odeum played out with the snooping faces of the men so obvious in their drools. They awaited sheepishly to hear her sweet voice, but none came, as only Bhaskara answered the dart of questions even as he grabbed the bride's hand and tried to make way into the small crowd of men, women and children.

The women grew wary of their men – their eyes sobered and excitement quelled. They discussed amongst themselves the probable palimpsests of motives and circumstances behind the alliance, the nativity of the bride, and how Bhaskara came to be a part of such a situation. "It is too early!" they declared in hushes. "Who marries within three months of a wife's passing? Moreover, why did she, of great beauty, agree to marry a widower? Maybe something is wrong with her, they whispered, sliding their bodies against the dried-up algae wall. A widow? An orphan? Or probably incapable of carrying a child?" One said she might be mute since she had not spoken a word at all. They couldn't understand. She was a stranger after all. And such, the new bride became venison for the colony's garbed carnivores.

Bhaskara's eyes quelled, brought upon by this chaotic drivel of unforeseen attention. His mind lost itself in an afterthought of an act he had committed in lustful desire. Although uninteresting, his first wife had been just as common as him and they had had a self-sustaining setup. Between them, he had held a higher place as he had a social position and she had been a "mere homemaker". But the attention on his new bride began to disrupt his recently established gloat about having gotten a beautiful wife, which, between them, had quipped an interest. As soon as he realized that it was being perceived as an unequal marriage, he let go of her hand, and the sudden drop clamored her glass bangles against each other, sliding down onto the ends of her wrist in a dirty uncertainty. A treble of disharmony struck his once-triumphant win— it now unraveled itself as a liability and unleashed a riot on his ego, which had been beefed up like a sheep for sacrifice by his underdog of a first wife.

Some elders of the colony, who still held their sanity, spoke of the disadvantage. They augured a painful path ahead for Bhaskara. All eyes were going to be on her. When the slow walk to their house ended, the new bride acknowledged the hospitality, after a rather visibly hard nudge by her husband. Everyone heard her sweet voice, and the women concluded she was not mute. Nobody asked her name, but the old woman said she must be a Parijatha, one of celestial birth. The old woman also said a woman leaves her name behind after marriage and acquires a new name in her husband's life. So, henceforth she would be called Parijatha.

Eyes followed Parijatha wherever she went, gauging her every move—a stranger still in so many ways. Men ogled shamelessly, their thoughts bereft of sonder, and talked to her on the behest of asking her innocent questions about her life. Dishes began pouring in from the neighborhood on the pretext of sharing when only they wanted to grasp a smell of her shadows, and this continued throughout the week. The men secretly compared her with the dead first wife who was, in all her essence, just like the other women of the colony, who continued to be alive—rotund, unkempt, greasy women. But not Parijatha. She had struck like a plague. A plague they welcomed with swooning hearts. Bhaskara was not extraordinary; he was a bald, average-looking man. The men openly teased Bhaskara of how lucky he was, with generous, outpouring libido in their eyes and unrestricted mouths grinning in imaginative, wild ecstasy.

The women slowly grew from resentment to a fit of spiteful jealousy, cursing the beauty that had befallen their lives. They knocked their knuckles and spit needlessly to their sides as Parijatha walked past them. The most affected were the immediate women-neighbors who lived constantly under her succinct but upsetting shadow. She was looked at like a wolf awaiting its prey, tormenting their very existence.

Meanwhile, Bhaskara changed rapidly, avoiding colleagues and people in general. And most of all, he began to lock up his wife when he left for work. The poor girl, after finishing her chores, sat by the window sill, scrambling for some sunlight, her hands either knitting or eyes gazing at the playing children, until her husband returned to unlock the door. She would hurriedly close the window at the sound of the motor jeep that echoed through the hills as he drew closer to the house. She would then run inside to immerse her hands in clearing vessels or washing clothes. He began to bring the groceries, vegetables, and even garments home, so she didn't have a reason to step out. And occasionally when he took her out after her howling fight that she cannot live caged like this, he took her far away where there was nobody who knew them – maybe the viewpoint by the ledge of the dam or its backwaters, or the adjacent village where you found fresh fish. On those nights they made love.

Bhaskara continued to speak, but only tangentially avoiding any kind of interest expressed in his personal life. And on the days people probed him anything, he would go and beat his wife over reasons as silly as she breathing in air.

For Parijatha, very soon the passing days became non-directional just like walking silhouettes in darkness, she did not know if they were approaching or parting. And sometimes it was weeks before anyone even caught a glimpse of her. The women sighed in temporary relief. Bhaskara grew distant, came home late and drunk, woke her up if she was sleeping and abused her until she cried her eyes out to sleep. There came a time when Parijatha didn't want to go out and began wanting to stay indoors.

Like a forbidden fruit beckons more desire, the men began to discuss her even more in her absence, imagining what she might be doing and where she was from based on her skin tone, her silky-straight hair. Some felt sorry for her state and advised Bhaskara not to lock her up like a chained animal, which he only misunderstood as them causing trouble in his life. Other men began to ignore their wives, and with dissatisfied minds and disgruntled void in their hearts, dismissed their call for help in daily chores, "You are not a damsel from the heavens, do your work." They secretly thought of their wives as tarnished by the colony's coastal terrain, by heat and humidity, too local and unintelligent to know anything of the world outside; that they were utterly monotonous and lifeless creatures walking on the face of this earth, who only harangued the men in monotones of fixated drudgery. So they cursed themselves for not having looked beyond the horizon while marrying.

About a few months later, a Wednesday weighing on the morning air, raged a silent remorse. A morose fuss filled the firmament as if it was out and about for a good hunt. And soon, the news fell into everyone's ears – from the milkman, the maids, the vendors, the loitering workers, the echoing chirps of the birds, the traversing clouds, the lonely street dogs, unattended stray cows, the empty window and the fluttering curtain behind it with nobody to tuck them – the news fell – that Parijatha had killed herself. The house and the streets were immersed in silence, only broken by the occasional cries of unaware infants. Everyone gathered to see her. The women kept a watchful eye on their men, for they were not certain if her death could succeed in keeping a check on their madness.

Men asked Bhaskara if anyone had to be informed of it, someone close to her to get a final glimpse of this woman forlorn. And when nobody came, the women attended to the inner details of readying Parijatha's body for the last rites. In accordance with the customs, they seated her half-naked body and took turns to pour holy water. They spoke of the motives behind her decision – an evil play of the charlatan fate, a layered game played by the politics of the society or was it the stowed-away, twisted ego of a man that emerged in spasms of abuse?

"Even the flowing water remained untainted," one of the women remarked. They asked for her wedding saree and dressed her in the same red tussar silk she had draped when she arrived first, applied a big imperfect round of vermillion on her forehead. She looked resplendent as ever as they laid her down, decorated her with the ornaments and applied turmeric on her cheeks, arms and feet. She was only marred by an imperfection marked by death, which had painted her lips purple, but left a gape of final peace on her mouth. Nobody yet knew who she really was or where she came from. Slowly women began to express their sympathy, blaming the men for their constant interference, meddling mouths. To be under the persistent gaze of an arsenal of prying eyes. Some women thought they could have done more to not alienate her when she was alive, as they slid their bodies against the felty, algae-ridden green walls, causing an irretrievable stain. Even in death, Parijatha's body shone against the wet, green-brown earth, as they lowered her body for burial.

Many months later, many, many Wednesdays later, Bhaskara came back again after time broke out of sympathy, of overwhelmed episodes, and when days broke open from the shell of old, estranged memories. He brought another wife – bland, rotund, familiar face and more suited to the demographic interests of the colony. Children gathered around, pulling their hands, running to their mothers, coy and shy at a stranger. She said she was just from the adjacent village. Men looked from behind the glass panes of the lifeless hotel, laborers constructing tar road (the first time tar was being put in the colony), looked intermittently at the couple from behind the road roller. Women stood with their backs against the dry walls. Somewhere, the cockerels crowed in disgust at human exuberance and inane madness, and one of the women remarked, "I wonder if these tarred roads are capable of surviving the torrential coastal rains."

Lotus Staircase

When I came to my senses, I found myself in a strange place. I knew it was 12 a.m. on early Wednesday; I always remembered Wednesdays. It was still dark outside. Much stranger was the fact that I had been awake all along, and I did not recall when I descended into all this—this, which looked like a giant well, sort of a spiral stairway. I looked up and around. All still a blur. There was no energy left to panic. Moreover, I was used to closed spaces now, especially after Bhaskara began to lock me in. "You still have a lot of room to move around," he'd say.

Everything weighed me down heavily, as if an up or outside of me never existed. Everything collapsed into me, like a black hole. My dismayed calls were weak and intransigent. I looked around again and realized I was right in the center of this enormous spiral stairway. The rigid trellis ran from the bottom of the stairwell to the top along the giant stanchion. There were climbing plants all along, woven together densely, which left little to no room to see the end of this stairwell. I found a tiny gap and peeped, and I could see that it was designed to be a blooming lotus from the aerial view, and down below, I saw the heart of the lotus.

Even in my agony and an all-encompassing indifference I found it beautiful! But what I saw was all hazy and dream-like, and I made a lazy note to understand it better at a later time. Perhaps someone could explain it to me, for according to Bhaskara, I was a dud and failed to understand most things most of the time.

The trellis openings were too small to see anything more, and as I peeped in every gap, only one half of it would be lit while the other half drowned in darkness. I checked another opening; it was the same. Startled, I sprung back. I couldn't tell for sure, but I was half way down this staircase. The more I tried to recall, the more my memory evaded me, and I couldn't remember how I had descended into this. It was probably days after my arrival here in the colony.

A panic set in for no reason and my heart raced. I felt heavy, but I gathered myself and tore into some creepers, butted my head out to look below the newel. It was abysmal. At the center of *that* dancing darkness, a small light twinkled like a star. I looked up to find the exit, which would lead me again to the surface. It was way high up and appeared like a small, blissful halo from where I stood. I could see the tumultuous blue night sky, tweaked by the vividness of trees, birds snug in their nests, and floating shrouds of clouds. Palling sounds of civilization would soon fill upon daybreak. Grass spiked along its circumference. The creeper thrust me back in and closed itself up as I collapsed. I tried to get up, I wanted to get out but collapsed on one of the steps. I realized there were stones tied to my ankles, my knees, a band of weights across my waist, my arms, my neck, and a turban of weight on my head. Moving was impossible. Who would do such a thing? It was a decadence which I had inflicted upon myself. My marriage to the wrong man and an indictment by the others for being beautiful. An insight lit up and the more I pondered over it, a strange pitiful indulgence began to set in. I loathed myself, obsessing over my sad state, yet distancing from the situation like it was someone else. My heart wept in a routine dreariness.

After a while, I lost any ability to think and I gave up. Everything became robustly blank. A mat of darkness spread itself on my heart and mind. And slowly, it was hunting down all the segments of happiness and hope that remained. Despite all this happening, there was not even an effort from inside of me to reconcile with my stumbling intelligence. I let it happen as if it were not my concern anymore. Tired and overwhelmed, I slept on the nearest landing, hoping it was a bad dream and that when I woke up again, I would find myself on my bed, in the house where my husband locked me. My husband, Bhaskara, who was unaware of my whereabouts. And I had to get out before my absence angered him further.

I don't know how much time passed, as time had lost all its meaning, but when I woke up again, the sun was about to appear in sight. I sought the sunrays not so much to relish them but to activate my consciousness for a clear, reasonable mind. I am a practical person, and for all reasons known and unknown, I thought I should try to get out of here. So, I gathered bits of myself and decided to have a plan. I tried to hoist my logic, reasoning, and intelligence. I looked around thoroughly and tried to know my surroundings. It was a staircase, alright! I had never seen anything like it. It took the proportions of an entire tornado; resplendent and grand with thick metal stalks of vines for balusters. Each baluster had a pink bud on its top that popped out of the railing, and from the previous stalk, a branch connected to the next baluster, making it all look like a part of a giant vine. Each one as tall as a fully-grown tree. The stairs were big, roomy, and had bed-like steps of Calacutta marble. I pulled myself up and butted my head out of the creepers again to see what the abyss looked like. I saw that a few flights below, the stairs had developed plants, weeds, and thorny shrubs, making it difficult for anyone who tried to get past that point.

I made efforts to climb up, but with everything weighing me down, believe me, I could just cross half a stairway. Mild sounds of clatter resounded – approaching heels of a pair of shoes against the floor, water trickling, lip smacking, or the jingling of trinkets. Tired and dazed, I sat down. I recalled all the incidents in the colony, how the men drooled over me, how Bhaskara changed drastically, nitpicking on me over the silliest of things. I felt depressed and dead.

Suddenly, a young man came climbing down. He walked right past me as I sat with my head reclined to the baluster with all the weights weighing me down. He didn't want to look at me, and I didn't want to look at him either. He was lanky and had more weights on him than his body could handle. His hair rested on his head like a mangled bunch of wires, and his black shirt hung on him like it would on a hanger. He himself looked like a tattered piece of cloth, unkempt, shabby, and wasted. There was a badge on his arm that seemed to belong to a cult. He climbed the steps down hurriedly, almost rolling like a ball in an alley, and disappeared quickly. I listened until I could no longer hear his footsteps. I could sense that it was a pernicious predicament to what was happening. I waited; my mouth had dried up, but there was no willingness to quench it. After a while, I peeped through the gaps of the baluster, to see what became of the young man, and I could see that he seemed willingly trapped and exhausted in one of the weedy bushes further down.

In a while, a striking young woman came walking up the stairs, and it soon became clear that the heels that made sounds all morning were hers. Her weights seemed to be lesser than mine, and she seemed faintly happy. *A survivor*, I thought. A distant smile lingered on her, but she beamed like a warrior returning from a battle she had won. Her eyes spoke of a mature despair of unseen battles that were yet to come.

"As you go deeper, the weights will increase and there you might reach a point where you might feel really helpless and plunge yourself to the heart of the Lotus."

"What happens then?"

"You are dead. You become one with that star. However, if you are strong and want to fight and have the willingness to live, the weights reduce slowly. And as they reduce you can gradually find your way up and reclaim your life."

"What is this place?" I asked her.

"This is a depression stairwell"

"But it's so beautiful!"

"Ha. You are the first person to be saying that. Probably because living here has made you happier than living outside of here."

"What happens if I don't plunge myself?" I asked.

"You go deeper and deeper until it eats you up. The weights will make sure of that," she said.

The striking lady continued to climb up slowly, but persistently like a solider in a troupe, one step at a time and remarkably the weights seemed to be coming down too. She sat down leaning on the baluster. She still had a lot to climb to reach the surface. She unfurled her snood and began to fan herself and ate something she was carrying.

She sure is getting better, I thought, *for, I could not eat a morsel of food.* She sat there for a long, long time. I called out to her.

"What's it like up there?" I asked her.

"Oh, it's beautiful! It's not like the deserted barrenness from where you talk, nor like the hellish, thorned zone of the abyss. From here, I can hear the cheeps of the birds again, and the sounds of loved ones. Here I can feel. Here I can breathe effortlessly. I can feel the sun rays kissing!" her voice was so calm yet full. There was a wholesomeness, which I had long forgotten.

I sat there and thought about how I would feel if I were to get out. There was a slumber even in my open eyes. I could smell the whiff of the plant but not the fragrance of its flowers. The sun felt a burden and day and night merged into a void. The birds looked like motored machines. And the colors around me drained me and felt like an imposition. Why was it all necessary? Was it really what I wanted? To go back to a bitter life where other women looked at me like I was a disease? I felt tired and drowsy.

I slept again. I don't know for how long.

A sudden huge thud and a burst of scream startled me awake. Cries of a man had whizzed past, like a bellowing human train and he had fallen with the thud. A glorious light lit up the staircase. I waited for a while, to hear even a whimper of that same voice. Maybe he was alive? Soon cries of another woman filled the stairways, as she descended down the steps from the open air. She clenched her knees, quivering at each step. With tears rolling down her eyes, lips swollen, cheeks pale, and tumbleweed-like hair scattered to the wind, she wept, "My son, my son!" she cried in vain.

When she met the striking young woman who was on her way up, she asked desperately, "Have you seen my son?"

"No, but I saw him last night, leaning over the edge of the entrance. I tried to warn him, begged him to get back. But he didn't listen."

The mother began to descend further with more weights around her than she could handle. I sat across, my hands now holding the baluster. My baluster, trying to avoid the woman.

"My son, my dear son, is he here? Have you seen him? You couldn't have missed him; he has the most beautiful green eyes."

I did not answer her. I did not want to. I couldn't care less. My heart had turned into a stone. I looked away.

The woman, grasping her knees, limping in pain, and the stones accumulating over her, went down the steps in haste, in pursuit of her son, to be one with him. "I will climb down to eternity, I will dance on the fire in that hell till I find my son," she mumbled in tears, her rage flowing down the steps like a roaring river, like the haste of a hunter to catch the game. And soon, light lit up the entire staircase. The mother had become one with her son.

I looked down if anyone was coming up or if anyone had been climbing down. I looked up again to see if Bhaskara was looking for me, to help me out of this, to a promise of a better life. But alas, I knew the answer. My heart wept irreparably. As the dawn broke, the sky was filled with thousands of glittering stars. *Whatever*, I thought. The waning crescent moon glided past the circular firmament. Nothing seemed to evoke any feeling inside me, I wanted to not wake up. Ever. I plunged into the heart of the Lotus. The stairway ignited as I became one with the light.

Perils of a Priest

Most respected members of the Devasthanam Board, I, Guru Ramateertha, write in my capacity as a senior trustee of this glorious *mutt* to which I have rendered selfless service and dedicated my entire life. As you are all aware, over these years, I have taken it upon myself to recruit aspiring priests who come from villages near and far, nurture them, and pass on the knowledge, the working principles of the *mutt*. Today, they are all acclaimed to be well read, disciplined, and I guarantee they are competent to carry on their shoulders the responsibility of the *mutt* with utmost devotion and piety. Some have even achieved accolades as Sanskrit scions in various parts of the world. I am proud to take recognition that I have had the right eye to catch them early on. To this day not one of them has let me down. Not in 45 years of my service to this institution have I seen any lacuna in my sincerity, or had doubts that I could have done something differently. Except until yesterday. I *must* admit and deeply apologize for a mistake that I might have made in one such appointment. The ways of this particular priest may initiate a decay in the discipline of our system and end up corrupting the working of our establishment. Worse, he will bring more disgrace to our *mutt*. Hence it is my painful duty to bring to the notice of the board the actions of this man and request that it is imperative that you terminate this priest's association with the institution.

Late afternoon, on Thursday, I was heading to the *mutt* in my car. You all know how important Thursday evenings are, with the special pujas and services to the deity. I was driving past the moving theater near the post office and was taking a left at the beginning of a steep road, and my car jerked as I released the clutch a bit too early to accelerate. And just then, I saw a man on a bike coming from the other direction at full speed. He suddenly swerved his vehicle, as if he were at a chicane of a race track and hit my car. The veering was so sudden and nasty, my heart banged. His knees almost grazed the concrete road. The swerve was not an accident but a gimmick to scare the rider of the car—me, for causing a slight inconvenience. It had irked him that a car had suddenly stopped and was in his way. He wanted to "give it back". He almost knocked off Ms. Saroo Gouli, who was unassumingly walking by the side of the road, probably heading to the village after her weekly deposit at the post office. The man finally screeched his bike to a stop about a hundred feet ahead while I sat still at the wheel, in a mix of terror and angst.

Oh, he looked towards the car alright! His demeanor was one of retaliatory satisfaction. My car has tinted glasses, so I am sure he didn't see who was inside. At my age, one gets easily shocked and takes much more time to gather oneself under such overwhelming circumstances. So, I drove the car slowly and parked my car by the side of the road to let it all sink in. Once I calmed down, I gathered all my energy and got out of the car, my legs still trembling, and turned around to take a good look at the biker. The man was collecting Saroo's dispersed post office documents and evidently pretending an apology as he handed them over to her. It was then that I actually noticed this man. His head was covered in a helmet, but his sacred thread was flying in the wind, fighting against his bare chest hair, and then there was sandalwood paste on his body. The *dhoti* he wore had the logo of our *mutt* embroidered along the border. There was no missing the body hair, for it was dense over the back of his shoulders. It became clear to me that he was Swami Padmanabhan. For a moment, I cursed myself to have doubted such a man of piety, told myself it probably was an accident, and that it could happen to anyone who's taking a steep turn at a crowded corner. The evening prayer time was nearing, and he probably was heading to the market to purchase some materials for the *puja*.

But what followed put my doubts to shame. *I shall talk to him when I meet him at the temple later*, I thought. The man took to his bike again and I got into my car too. As soon as I started my car, a big roar from the bike thundered across the entire stretch. What I saw in the rearview mirror, my Lord! Swami Padmanabhan was wheeling his bike! You can imagine my horror! Here was a man clad in all things meant to effuse godliness and a purpose to rhapsodize reverence from a community in a public space! And he was wheeling! Everyone nearly jumped at the raving sound, especially the elderly who always throng the post office for an evening chat. And everyone recognized him to be from our *mutt*.

An irreparable shame has been brought on the name of our institution by the deplorable acts of this man. I request the board to take immediate cognizance of this act and bring Swami Padmanabhan to the stands. I take the entire responsibility for bringing this upon the institution. A poor judgment. Such profanity should be condemned with the harshest measures, and this should set an example for other priests.

Thanking you.
Yours respectfully,
Guru Ramateertha

Vengeance of the Broken Wing – A Chronicle

I Gateway of fatal feather

"We are living in various places now, the three of us; scattered by the deceptive undulations of time. When we reconnect, we talk about it," Sethu Laksmi said, still in wonder of the unearthly occurrence of 20 years ago lingering in her voice. An episode carved like an occult filigree by an indiscernible power. "Now, modernity has taken over," she said as she sat down. "There's hardly any room for anyone to assign a favorable credibility for such an occurrence." Strange as it is, of the many written and vocal folklore, most of them have remained just that. Folklore. But not this. So when Sethu Laksmi agreed to talk about it, I was ecstatic.

The path, that leads to the *Gateway of the fatal feather*, as it was called, was talked of several times by everyone I met, and when I, like several other passers-by crossed it, it was emphasized, with an evident enthusiasm and recollections narrated with arms in the air. A legendary beholder of a divine energy in the colony's anthology, it was hailed as one of its sundry glories.

"The older men have magnificent narratives passed down over generations. They cajole your imagination and give a narrative as old as the mythology itself. And we were no different, the same was told to us every night by our parents and grandparents," Sethu Laksmi said as her eyes fell on the magnificent portrait that hung to her left. The servant woman came down quietly and sat on the floor next to her. She elaborated further, "The wing that was felled, they say, was as big as a mountain and the barbs as dense as the thickets of the ghats and the magnitude, if one might ask, was beyond what the pale faces and cloistered eyes could fathom. That when it fell from the sky in a swirl of its own, it shook the wind around it to such enormous gusts that a tornado formed, uprooting the enemy villages who had plundered the women of their village. The place you ask, they say it fell in the middle of the forest, (now a grove) creating a crater as an asteroid would, falling from such great heights even the strictures of galaxies couldn't hold it. Have you ever heard of a wing so mighty as to create a dent in the earth? The crater which held the humungous wing eventually subsumed it into its own bosom."

As I listened with unfettered attention, she asked me with a gasping fervor to guess who the wing belonged to, and almost immediately replied, her eyebrows raised in disbelief, "The mighty Jatayu! The slain fighter! Felled by the beastly king who lacked virtue."

I could immediately grasp the portrait which adorns the walls of every home here. Jatayu, the bird slain, his eyes filled with devotion even in death, prostrating in front of a very collected Lord Rama. The servant offered *namaskarams* to the portrait at Sethu Lakshmi's narration.

Sethu Laksmi slowly opened up in her quivering voice, "I can still taste the feathers in my mouth and often do in my dreams, only to wake up spitting in shots all over my duvet. Like I said, we had grown up with these stories, and Jatayu protecting the women was an integral part of the womenfolk in the colony. However, over time they had become archaic until *this* episode happened. It was as if *He* wanted to revive himself from the threat of being forgotten. Ours was the first in a long time!" she said. The servant nodded heavily, "And after that, there were many more instances of retributions."

I had checked and many in the colony agreed – women incapacitated by abuse, mangled in spirit, tousled in their treads of gaiety, went offering prayers for an although unequal justice, or in a lackluster hope that karma will serve its futile course, for there was no undoing the done. The instances witnessed concluded in chimerical ways of justice. Even an ephemeral, but reasonable retribution to the unaccountable action and salacious attempts of their wrongdoers.

"A death knell if a man wronged a woman," said the older woman, bringing us all some tea.

II The day of the incident

Speaking of that eventful evening, Sethu Lakshmi continued, "It was not like we were minding our business in the middle of the grove that night. It was not a place to be at that time of the hour, not for young women like us. I had been married for a year. My husband was a policeman and failed to differentiate work and life like most policemen. He looked at everyone with suspicion, implemented his methods to the silliest of household follies, and used law and order ubiquitously on me. To a great extent, it became difficult to distinguish him from a common criminal." The servant woman looked upon Sethu Lakshmi in awe, like it was the first time she was hearing of it all.

"Neither Shakambari nor Medharathi were married. Shakambari lived with her grandmother having lost her parents at a very young age. She was the feisty one. Precocious. Never took no for an answer and never bowed down. She always tied her hair in braids of 3; had a thing for neem leaves and, as directed by her grandmother, collected them and used its essence in hot baths. So, she always smelled like it. On the other hand, Medharathi was hounded day and night by her older brother who worked as a truck driver and was away for every other fortnight. When he returned, he badgered her with questions of who she had been with, why she talked to a man on her way back, why her hair was not pinned up, or why she did not reach home before sunset. He tormented her and with it came beatings, whether or not her answers were valid. Eventually, Medharathi stopped answering his questions, and with it came more beatings. She and I connected well on these grounds."

The servant woman extended her long calf, exposing it as she dipped oil from a small steel bowl and began to knead her muscles, "Shakambari was always peculiar, *Akka*. Her entire family has always been shrouded in mysterious stories and tales. No one believed it all, until the episode."

"In those days, a new kind of oriental, boutique art had taken over all the young girls' artistic hinges. And on the morning of that day, Shakambari announced that she had signed up the three of us for a workshop. It was to take place at an inspection bungalow about 40 minutes away from the colony. By foot. It was not uncommon in those days."

"A forty-minute walk was not unheard of. We all walk to villages even now," the servant added.

"By afternoon, Shakambari took a warm neem-infused bath, and with her 3 braids set, waited cross-legged on the porch of her house. Her grandmother who was generally barely able to stand upright, was prancing in small steps to a song from the past. Her gray hair was tied in thin braids of 3 as well, and a girl of yonder had taken over her soul. Although she faced the road, she observed her grandmother's moves from an invisible eye on her back. As soon as we arrived, she got up, slid her feet into the slippers, swung her braids over her shoulders, and with the wind sticking out her body against her floral country co-ord skirt set, she pulled her 2 friends away from the show. Medharathi and I walked ahead, vying over our common woes as usual. Shakambari, never having had to live with any man of any role, showed obvious plaintive indifference to it."

"She hadn't seen what we had seen, she didn't know what it was like to have a man around," Sethu Lakshmi said. "And we never blamed her for that. Whenever we talked about it, she listened in silence or wandered a bit away from us and muttered to herself. Over a period of time, we realized the nature of these mutterings. She and her grandmother had the ability to sense things about each other. It was the strangest thing, like a mother's sense of her child. But only it was mutual. And *strong*."

"We later found out how strong, it is divinity itself!" the servant said with folded hands, as if the words and narrations themselves were to be revered.

"As we walked on that dust-ridden path by the side of the road, we heard Shakambari faintly mutter – '*Ajji* is fighting with Ramanna again.' Her head buried perpendicularly as she studied the soil, the pebbles that altered the pathway's color and texture. We paused, looked puzzled at each other and continued with our banter over men."

The servant woman got up to get more oil, and her voice echoed from an inside, dark room, "*Ajji* fighting with Ramanna was a thing of routine. The day before, Ramanna had teased *Ajji* about her tattoo."

"It was said that *Ajji* had a tattoo on the inner side of her right arm that read *Arunadri Acchappa*. She had lived in this colony all her life, but nobody had known an Arunadri or Acchappa or what her relationship with them was. Various theories had run their course roaringly around the colony for a long time – a long-lost love, an unborn child, abandoned kin. But several years later, in a very public gathering during a ritual when Ramanna had irked her with his loose-tongued misconducts, all hell had broken loose."

"She seethed in anger, thundering her answers to the questions of hundreds of mouths. 'You all have the same questions that just flow out in different voices – passive and active; subtle and crude'," the servant acted it out like *Ajji*.

"It was then that she narrated the incident when she had prayed and prayed to Jatayu for justice against the atrocities that she had faced under a certain Acchappa. And when her prayers were answered, she had etched the names of both her culprit and her savior, on the same skin of her arm which Acchappa had held. Acchappa, it seems, had deliberately held her hand in full public view to instill doubts about her character in the minds of people," Sethu Lakshmi said.

"Truth be told, many of them did not believe this story and continued to deride her," said the servant woman, as she sat down with an unease.

"Men had disliked her forthrightness and the women her free will. Women of her age even said she did not act as appropriate to her age, as *they* did. She did not involve herself in religious activities. And the men, when they gathered, gossiped about her, humiliating her with their insensitive references to her being a widow," Sethu Laksmi said.

"Coming back to *that* day, the three of us proceeded to the ghats. The sun had played in and out with the dense but scattered mass of clouds. It had been 3 weeks since anyone had witnessed a clear sky. When we just began to ascend the ghats, Eeshanna came heavily pedaling his bicycle uphill. His forehead was smeared in holy ash in entirety and adorned by a small vermillion dot at the center. He called out from behind, "Oo Shaku! *Ajji* is screaming at Ramanna again. He teased her about dancing at this age!"

"I looked at Medharathi, who was as startled as I! That was what Shakambari had been muttering all along. She had even been muttering abuses probably *Ajji* had been hurling at Ramanna!" Sethu Lakshmi continued, "We all felt an unease at his unexpected addressing her as *Shaaku.*

We didn't call her Shaaku! Only her grandmother did. Occasionally in endearment."

"Saying so, he paddled on, heavily thrusting his body to and fro against his cycle, and was soon out of sight. Back here, Shakambari only knew too well and began to recite verbatim the words of her grandmother – 'You useless man, your brain is cluttered only by cunningness to suck the joy out of women. Isn't that why your wife left you? Get lost before I jump and break your leg. Out!'" Sethu Lakshmi recounted.

"Once at the inspection bungalow, the workshop had already begun. We quickly found our places and forgot about Ajji and Ramanna or Eeshanna. Such workshops were novel to our remote colony, a concept we had never seen or heard of. The instructor was blurting out ways of giving an opaline effect. We stroked and heated the canvas for the best outcome. While Medharathi and I worked keenly, Shakambari was tense and began to mumble again in moans of despair – 'She's crying again. Her anklets kneading against the floor, her braids pressed against the wall of tarnish.' Her grandmother was in despair and Shakambari said she sensed something was about to happen. We finished the session with a disinterested detachment."

III The Trigger

"Despite the urgency and unease, Shakambari wanted to talk to the instructor what about no one knew. 'I'll be down in a minute, you both start,' she said to us."

"The tall pillars of the administration building looked taller against the afternoon cloud-set firmament. They had walked for about twenty minutes, when they heard Shakambari calling out to them to stop. They looked back and waved at her to come join them fast. 'At this rate, the night will set by the time I get home,' Medharathi was knuckling her fingers anxiously." "When Shakambari finally caught up, she narrated the horror. She had been walking on the usual route, hoping to catch up with the two of us, but the small stretches of roads between the hairpin curves made it impossible for her to catch a glimpse of us. She was pondering over the impulses of her grandmother, when suddenly someone had groped and squeezed her breast. She stood there in a moment of shock, trying to understand what had happened. A shooting pain had struck her breast. She looked up and *that* man was on the bicycle, peddling unperturbed and didn't look back, but she knew *that* bicycle; the bicycle that came to everyone's houses to collect the cable fees and the bicycle that had whizzed past them on their way up. 'It was Eeshanna!' she declared, sobbing. Shame-struck, teary-eyed, she continued, "'I ran as fast as I could, sometimes hoping to catch him and thrash him'."

"She thought of the things she could have done – chased him, punched him in that split second, knocked him off his cycle. She cursed herself for not standing up to this violation. We tried to pacify her. And after a while, everyone walked in silence. On descending the ghat, we stopped at the big highway. In front of us were two small lanes and one big road that led to the colony."

"And then Medharathi suddenly said, 'You know, the Jatayu gate is not far from here!' A flash of grim hope for a retribution descended. It was something we had heard in stories. The unpunished imbalance raged in all our eyes. Courage transcended immediately and occupied us. 'At least let's try. If nothing happens, nothing happens! I am tired of my abusive brother and she of her abusive husband'."

Sethu Laksmi was looking at the roof and dragged her words in contemplation, "I was just thinking, *Is it even true? Will it even work?* We hadn't even heard a single incident that said it was true. All of us had questions but Shakambari declared, 'Jatayu *will* do justice!' and we headed to the gateway. I remember not believing in the entire venture. I remember thinking of myself as too mature and practical to believe in it all, but I headed to the gateway anyway. They were my friends after all."

IV The Venture

"The time was 6 minutes to 5. Turbid neon lights lingered from the highway, from where we had walked, exactly a kilometer, and then turned northwest of the morass to reach the Jatayu grove – The *Gateway of the fatal feather.*"

When I had talked to the priest, he recalled that he was heading back from the gateway's shrine after the head priest took over for the rest of the evening. It was when he had just crossed the morass that he saw the girls and guided them to the grove. He had said, "And they rather replied rudely to me – *we know where it is!* I had also warned them to return before the wild animals set out, as only the preceding week some pug marks had been spotted about a kilometer west of the grove. But, my bad! The girls snubbed me and said they knew well what to do."

When I talked about the priest, Sethu Lakshmi and the servant said, "Oh! Some priest that man! Soon after he was dismissed by the grand seer, over some wheeling!" The evening got cold early on.

"The priest was trying to defy the formation of an octagon with a bundle of sacred thread. He was trying to align it to a sanctimonious 7, but somehow it kept falling into an octagon as if on a mission. When we looked back, we could see him just stepping on to the footprints left by us. *How perverse!* we thought to ourselves."

"Shakambari's eyes were still furious, a whimsical eagerness to get something done, with a magical spur in her belief that it was going to go as they thought. Strangely, as we walked, she recited phrases of what her grandmother was doing, prophetically. None of us knew the procedure, the invocation of a curse upon these men who had in some way caused us pain and suffering. If I think about it now, Shakambari was guided through her grandmother on what was to be done."

"As we stood there, caught in the howling cold wind, we too decided to put ourselves deeper into it and check if the stars aligned to help us in our overture of an uprising. We walked into the gateway, and as we stood there, where many people seemed to have stood before, we folded our hands. Soon, the dry dust was rising the tiny fireflies along with it, and a struggle began in an attempt to maintain direction. Ominously, a storm was brewing up. We learned later that the meteorological department had even issued out warnings. The K-colony was at the fringe of the purported area of the storm, but nonetheless, the effects would probably be experienced over the colony. We tried to find the head priest but he was nowhere to be seen. So we assumed he might have gone to collect some herbs from around as he usually did. We stood there looking up at this whirlwind of fireflies which seemed to be only getting more and more in number. Suddenly there was a big, loud sound of unheard magnitude. At first, we thought it might have been a disaster in the nearby dam. Our minds pondered about the right way to go about this ritual and our hearts pounded for vengeance. For retribution."

V Jatayu

"We didn't find it to be unsafe at that time, a feeling of 'someone guarding' swept the air. My big dome earrings dangled and the *ghungroos* lining up in the ends jingled in my ears like a stream of honeybees. Though it didn't unsettle the silence of the grove, its tintinnabulations and the fear thumping in our chests were all happening too close to think that they didn't perturb the surroundings. We wanted to disappear into the grove itself, to become so one with it that these sounds were no more external to the grove. The worry made our eyes heavy and spines feeble. Our bodies slowly defeated themselves and we fell like a pile of dried leaves discarded by a tree."

"Another loud sound. Everything looked hazy and the last of the evening rays danced with twists and turns; the clouds drooped and interspersed. They slowed the grove – the rays, the motley songs of the birds, the rustling of the dried leaves, the disappearance of the floating clouds, only to make way for a dense cumulonimbus. We could only see a vulture doing the rounds, up and high above like they usually do. But this one didn't look like a stranger or a nobody. It was familiar. But we couldn't be particular, our eyes were giving away. We rested our eyes for a moment or two – Was he a friend from the past? A savior? But his presence in the sky above the grove sent a sanguine radiance across the tumultuous confusion."

The servant added, "Meanwhile, Shakambari recited what her grandmother was doing back at her house."

Sethu Lakshmi continued, "Shakambari whispered to us, '*Ajji* is whisking the wickers, assembling the lamps, and lighting a thousand lights!' What happened next was disbelief! We looked up and saw *him* spiraling down, bringing with *him* the celestial elements that sent galactic sparks around *him*. Jatayu!"

"A tornadic gust brought about a sudden darkness. Everything around went blind except *his* wounded face that shone amidst all the magical charm *he* brought. *His* tarsus landed on the ground next to me with great perfection and *his* gigantic size rivaled even the hills so much so that *his* presence covered up the entire grove. *He* was wounded and what remained of *his* body was fast covering up with oozing blood. *His* beak too was soaked with blood and you could tell it was not his own. It had dried up, blocking his nares, and down at the mandibles they had formed little stalactites of scarlet. *He* was old and the bloody wetness inflicted upon his meager feathers bared much of his old skin underneath."

"Our bodies refused to get up. I stared at *him* in wonder from where I lay. I still couldn't understand the familiarity even as the sights in front of me harassed and teased my memory. *He* then began to rumble in tears. 'I couldn't...I couldn't!' he mumbled, his head down, defeated. There was a winsomeness even in all the pain. 'An old man that I am, I only have strength left to pick up morsels of food now, only enough strength to perch upon a prey, but not fight mighty rulers like him. Not anymore. Not like I did in my days. Lord save her!' His voice, demeanor all brought a feeling of home, of belonging."

"*He* heaved a sigh, tired from all the fighting, and continued in feeble voices, gasping in between brave pauses. 'He came rumbling across the forests, his ten heads destroying everything on his way, even the smell of earth. We came face to face. I tried to reason with him, that his actions were not befitting of a righteous man and he was much more than this. You know how he is. But he only ridiculed my age and scoffed at the virtues of which he had only heard from afar. I could only search in my memory for the reasonable man he once was.' He stopped to catch some air. Should we nurse him? His pain was all-pervading, even after so many thousands of years. We all looked at each other. The wounded giant continued –"

'He lashed out his sword which was studded with pearls and rubies and split the sun or so it seemed for there was no longer any light. He struck the Parijaata tree and felled all its flowers and the earth was devoid of any fragrance. His peals of laughter sent the animals, birds, and their little ones to the death knell. And there was no longer an air of melody. The gust of wind where once the nectar of flowers drizzled, now only left a taste of dust on the lips. Strings of sinful acts! Oh! where do I begin, where do I end.' His heart was doused in pain, and heartbreak danced in his eyes as he howled small gasps of cry. 'But…' his eyes dilated in a climatic gasp. 'I *had* to stop him! So, in a final attempt, I thrust my frail body with all those thousand years of learning weighing on my muscles and destroyed the chariot. I plucked away the beats on those horses and then it was the charioteer's turn, I plucked his head off with my beak,' he said with a final triumph. 'After losing them, I thought the beastly king would be left debilitated. Where would he go without his charioteer? But this man, now was driven by a desire so demonic, that he had turned into a phantom! And at that moment I saw madness conniving with might. I took the name of the goddess and charged at him with age and pain weighing me down heavily and shattered his bow and arrows. A thousand pieces of his ego went flying along with the remains of his godly equipment. He roared in anger.'"

"'I could see the devil in his eyes turning in on me. With a roar of a hundred lions and a sword in his hand, he jumped on the edge of the cloud he had chosen to fight me and then struck a blow on my wing. The agony was not from the inflicted wound, but that a man mighty and righteous once, could strike an old man as me, a king of the vultures, without the least reverence, for his words or age. My wing severed and fell on the hillock and so did all the pearls and rubies that adorned his sword. They splattered around my fallen wing and its feathers like jubilant little drops of dancing rain. And then I fell beside the wreckage, discarded by the forces of justice. I saw what the coming days would mean. The great war was imminent. I did all I could to prevent it, for my Lord.' And he looked at us, tears brimming on the edges of his beady eyes, over his failure to keep an untold promise, over his failure to protect the queen. He was the king of his kind. But now a mere animal, lying helplessly, in death. Helpless and alone."

"And suddenly when we woke up, there was nobody around, but an air of familiarity of an episode that still vexed our minds. The grove had caught a wisp of the vulture king in its air. We got up and began to walk back, tracing our steps. Shakambari muttered many a thing on the way back. But we were too dead to pay any heed."

"The next morning, news spread. Reporters came down from the town to report what they quipped as a fantastic accident of the decade. 'In an unusual occurrence, near twilight, a nearly blind vulture swooped down from its roost and in its hysteria hit a cycling man near the highway.

The adornments of his cycle and the wheels caught his feet. And the bird got trapped in a string of pearls the cycler had around his neck. The hysteria soon turned maniacal and the blind bird began to peck him. During this broil, an inter-state heavy vehicle ran over him. And the blind bird flew away at the faint hint of truck headlights, leaving the dead man dragging under the wheels of the vehicle for two hundred meters,' the reports said."

"Medharathi and I rushed to Shakambari's house, panic in our eyes. 'My brother was driving *that* vehicle! It was his last day at the timber corporation. He was about to join the state transport next month,' Medharathi gasped in a wild mix of emotions. 'The police have taken him away.'"

When I asked Sethu Laksmi about her husband, she said, "My husband didn't return home after that evening. Some said he went and joined the timber mafia after *that* truck was seized. They found contraband. He had been doing illegal activities."

When I contacted Medharathi to know what she thought of it, she said she remembers the dream vaguely and cannot assure me completely if it happened. But she said, "Yes, there was such a death." Nobody knows where Shakambari or her grandmother are now. Word has it that she has a tattoo of *Anjanadri Eeshappa* on her chest.

Unfinished Business

Amma has been in an indefinite vegetative state for a couple of months now. I could see the ventilator over her face go up and down as she breathed in elaborate respites. When I was 6, she left me in the care of her parents. My grandparents consoled me although I was not bawling over it or anything. I knew she'd be back. She would never abandon me. But it felt a bit unnatural and untimely. And the wait was getting rather tiresome.

Much time passed as I waited. In the mornings, I played in the garden, stomping over my muddy dams, blowing soap bubbles in the water wreckage. *Amma* had some work, but it was ok. She would be back. I rallied the clay bullock carts on the aisle that led to the grand white gate, back and forth, often peeping through the narrow crevices of the gate. Although the gate was grand in structure, it had corroded over the years around the edges of the square grill that formed the body of the gate. Grandfather had covered the mesh-like part with a thick, white polythene sheet, for privacy. So usually, I found gaps around the corners. I looked at the far ends of the road to see if there was a rickshaw that was heading my way. I then ran to the other end of the gate to catch a glimpse of the *other* end of the road; perhaps she had chosen to walk as the rickshaws usually refused to ride further in from the busy main roads. But all I could see was the July winds whirring up the dust. I didn't care. She would come home soon. She would be waiting to get back to me as much as I was waiting to get back to her. She would come and hold me and kiss my marble-like eyes. Like she always did.

I went back to play some cricket with my grandfather in the garden. The garden was not much but had layers of flowering plants. The short marigolds formed the front row along the aisle that led to the gate. *That* big white gate I told you about. And in the next row were a lot of rose plants. Mainly pink and white ones, all in full bloom but neglected as nobody had bothered to pick them. Had *Amma* been here, she would pick one and adorn her bun every day. At the far end, in a corner, was the jasmine vine which had grown so big and tall that we needed a ladder to climb up to pluck the buds. Grandfather hoisted the ladder in the evenings and I would climb up to pluck the buds. It was our thing. But for now, we stood under it as he bowled and I batted. I am not sure he enjoys it. He thinks it's a chore as he has to run and search for the ball among the bushes every time I hit. He does it at the behest of my grandmother; I once overheard her telling him. And I need someone to throw the ball too. Once Mumma comes, *she* will play with me. She always throws the ball to me when I want to bat. And she enjoys looking for the ball in the bushes; she says she can smell the scents of the flowers and spot insects too. When it gets dark, we play frisbee. Grandpa gets tired easily! No more than ten throws and he gets up to clear out the fronds of the coconut tree. He will clear out the dried leaves and make a broomstick out of the sticks.

I forgot about *Amma* for a while, as I played more in the mud, building clay toys for myself. I made some soldiers, a farmer, a pair of cow and calf. I dug a pond to make a paper boat later. I took some water from the pot and poured it in to see if it held water. It did. After I was done, I arrayed them all under the late afternoon sun to dry them up. That way they would be ready by the time *Amma* returned. And we could paint it together. Meanwhile, Grandpa finished making the broomstick and he called me out to pluck the jasmine buds. I climbed up and down as I plucked a handful of buds and put them in the silver basket that Grandpa held up against the ladder.

After a while, I went and stood near the grand gate again. Many passed about, but I kept all my senses open to know about Mother. I stood there alone, staring at the muddy road for a long time. There was nothing left to do but wait. Until Grandmother came and took me inside, "Come, Pari. Now now, she will be here soon."

Dusk brought loneliness and helplessness. It was the hardest time. I wandered about the house, searching for her in the fleeting shadows and ghosts, dragging my feet from room to room – in the closet, under the bed, a trinket, a freshly smeared lipstick, a scent. All of it in its entirety failed to add up to her. My heart wiggled like a dying fish. I wish I knew where she was, so I could run to her to fetch her *home*.

At nightfall, Grandma brought in dry clothes and dumped them on the sofa. "The cold, wild wind will make it soggy," she said. From its edge, the balloon-sleeves of *Amma's* blouse hung down like a dead person's arm. It smelled of detergent interspersed with dill leaves. I grabbed it and when nobody was around, smelled it, hugged it and shed a tear in silence and secret. We were tethered. Surely, she was listening to my silent calls, my whispers, and yearning.

I sought my grandmother's lap. But there was no indulgence. It only felt a bit like Mother's. Grandmother probably sensed my despair. She caressed my head, pressing her palm against my right temple as she did, to soothe me.

"Come, *Amma*!" I cried.

"She will come, my dear child. She will soon." And she whispered, "I do not know if I have to pray for her to live." I do not remember when I fell asleep. I could only hear my own sobs as I dissolved myself into an unknown.

The night passed, and in the early hours of the morning, a dead electronic monitor beeped in shrieks at the hospital. Grandma woke me up to it. After a while, the grand white gate creaked. I ran out to the door, rubbing my drowsy eyes, still holding onto the balloon-sleeved blouse. I saw my mother in all her glory, smiling upon me. She ran to me as I ran to her. She hugged me and kissed me, remarking how she had missed my marble eyes. "At last, we meet, my darling. There's no place I'd rather be," she cried to the heavenly skies.

A Suspect

The station was abuzz with the chit-chat of the college-goers who had assembled to go back home. They all came from a remote colony that had very few educational institutions. The gossip of housewives coalesced with the soaring silence of loners, whose eyes struggled to catch hold of just *that* one thing in their midst that could disengage their loneliness. The afternoon weighed heavily on everyone, but didn't quite seem to deter the talkers' drying mouths; for there was so much to be told and gossiped about and there was so little time. The mild, restless pigeons on the open ceilings of the station bobbled their heads in pauses as if shifting their attentions to the human drama beneath them. Occasionally, silences converged into a single, greater, big afternoon silence. It was then that the pigeons broke the air with a *coo roo c'too coo*. All part of a grand design.

The keepers swept and mopped the floors like it was the only thing in the world, robotically dipping the stick in a bucket of already-muddy water and swinging the bristles of it all along the granular-looking floor as they moved backwards and then onto the steps leading downstairs. Nobody seemed to bother about them. However, they did look up during those greater silences, breaking their own monotony – as if to assure that they were still humans, still alive. They seemed to catch a whiff in the wind when a peculiar-looking person came along – a hippy or a kink or a rare saint amongst the waiting crowd. All this as their hands continued to swing the mop across the floor and as passengers jumped past the long, ragged cloth that tossed about like ocean weeds on the shoreline.

A thin, short man sat on a square block of cement lined with granite—one of many such blocks on the platform—staring down at the floor in silence. He was deeply engrossed in the inlays of the fine granite that had become prominent under the glare of the sun. At the same time, he seemed lost in other thoughts, fixating on a trail of thin air much above the granite. His eyes bore a particular sadness, as if forced upon him, as if in his own crooked attempt to gather compassion through sad eyes and downward-tilted lips, but also looked eager to break it all and burst into happiness at the slightest chance.

He looked mushy and swollen around his eyes, and anyone would easily conclude that the man was high on dope or something. He was probably in his forties, but his old-school rectangle metal-framed glasses, gray hair, and blackened lips made him look older than he actually was. He wore a blue and white striped shirt that was half-tucked in irresponsibly and a pack of cheap *beedis*, half used up, snuck out of his breast pocket. The ends of the last few that remained looked like a cat's burned tail end. His top two buttons were undone, exposing his gray chest hair that flogged heavily on his skin under the might of the afternoon westerlies. This was paired with worn-off gray pants that were barely held up and muddied around the buttocks and feet, where it met the earth, leaving the hemming fighting for its very survival. One sharp blow of the wind ruffled up his cropped hair, adding to the already prevalent disorder in him.

He woke up to the humble announcement of the station that left sooner than it came. Its echoes were drowned in a burst of laughter by a group of students, conspicuously timed with the announcement. He turned his head to the speakers to listen more intently. He strained every muscle on his face and tightened his dopey eyes, batting his eyelids, yet maintaining the sadness in them. Most of the words went unheard, and he failed to grasp those one or two crucial pieces of information about the train—like the time of arrival or the platform number. He turned to the digital display board, which read that a train was arriving in the next 2 minutes at the platform that he was waiting on. In a moment, the sweet echoes from the announcer came again, "Please stand away from the yellow line." He got up to join the nearest queue that was beginning to swarm. There were disorganized queues. Like ants lining up to cubes of sugar, they lined up, each leading up to a door of the train that was about to dock. He smiled at a student girl in his line but was met with coldness. Changing times had brought anonymity, where once familiarity bred. And crimes were on the rise, breeding more mistrust, suspicion, avoidance than friendly exchanges.

The man picked up his off-white muslin bag that was all dirty at the bottom and the sides, pulled it up his shoulders, and pushed it further inwards a couple of times, to make sure it didn't slip, at least not until he found a place inside the train. As soon as the train was in sight, he turned back around and asked a young boy behind him, "This goes to Bonccu Garden?" he asked. The boy said, "Yes," dismissively, engrossed in his phone. Another older man beside him said, "But, you have to change trains."

He moved around swiftly without any qualms or confusion. He was neither new to the city nor new to commuting by the train. The train was full, and he didn't find any empty seats until after a couple of stops. Once he sat down, he placed his bag in between his legs on the floor. He looked around cluelessly once he settled down, and you wouldn't know if he were searching for something or wanted to find something that interested him. He brushed his hand up and down the joist that was by his side. The bustle didn't mellow down, for the students continued to yap about teachers and other students; then there was a man who played his radio obscenely loud, and the sound of his songs couldn't escape the barred doors and even mixed with the music seeping out of another student's headphones. The man stared out of the window for a while, looking lost, and then turned his back on the window. The sun was on his side of the window, and the constant energy burned his back and made it feverishly hot.

At the next stop, a mother and her four-year-old daughter came on board. The girl frolicked around ceaselessly, like she could do it all day and it was her only job and her mother struggled to get her composed enough to walk through the unreliable doors of the train – "Rhea, stop dancing around. C'mon. Come soon!" She pulled her indifferent child hurriedly.

The woman was like many other young mothers. She tried to hide her aging and traditionalistic nuances under the wraps of modern clothes. She conversed with her child in English. Tradition, however, had refused to leave her, for it was discernible in every last bit of her element – her selection of bangles that jingled at the end of her wrists, in the circle of her small vermillion between her thick bushman eyebrows, a circle so small it almost looked like a scar. There was no seat left to sit, so her mother held onto her and stood leaning on a pole. The girl was excited and ready to be entertained by the train ride she was about to have. The beetling ends of her romper shorts brought in cuteness and she soon got engrossed in counting its paisley prints – "W-one, to-ov, thee-e, fiie…" – her 2 ponytails tied meticulously by her mother pranced about to her vigorous nodding as she counted. The lonely passengers were left momentarily amused by the innocence and tenderness the little girl brought to their otherwise dull journey. They carried on with their businesses after a while, when the girl too started to seem dull and mundane. As the stops came, a few people left and more people came and the girl struggled to keep still.

The thin man, who was seeing all this without taking his eyes off the child, grabbed her thoughtlessly and suddenly and placed her on his lap – "Ah, come, little one, you can sit here with me!" he exclaimed, grinning at the little girl, taking his neck down to face her, his blackened lips spread across his narrow cheeks in a dubious grin. The girl continued with her babbling and counting, apathetic to her host who was now trying everything in his capacity to grab her attention. But she neither realized nor cared about being taken a little away from her mother, onto a stranger's lap. The mother was unable to ascertain it to be an act of kindness. She was thinking and calculating, and thinking again much beyond. She called out to her daughter to come to her, but Rhea was happy to get a view out of the window and refused to go to her.

Such a strange man! The mother remembered her younger days when she used to sit on stranger's laps – when *her* mother took her on the bus, but that was much, much before. Surely, this was one such act. But again, she knew she had always sat on women's laps, never men's. Who was this man! She studied him while he looked outside the window, with her daughter still sitting on his lap. She saw him running his dirty hands onto his bare chest, scratching it through all the curly, gray chest hair. After a while, he ran his hand onto his own thigh that was free from the child and rubbed it up and down.

She called out to her daughter again and the little girl refused yet again. The mother did not know what to do, for the man was unconvincing in his appearance, and looked more and more dubious now. He was unkempt, seemed to possess a questionable character and was possibly a pervert. It was hard to trust strangers in these times. He is definitely not a homely clerk! What if he is not looking at her with the right intention? Where is he holding her? What if he attempts to do something, trick her in the blink of an eye? She watched him like a hawk and swiftly led her eyeballs away when he came close to meeting her in the eye. He was trying to smile at her, and that was again questionable to her. There were men like him, men who seeped into the civility like maggots and brought decadency slowly, at an opportune moment. She studied him further; he was happy and smiling, and was putting on a show to please the child. *What if it is to divert attention or to befriend her*, she thought.

The train was heading to the underground after the next stop. She began to worry he might use the situation to his advantage. She had to do something and quick. She cursed herself for having taken the train today, and her heart started to pound. "Mumma, look at the cows! Mumma, cows down there!" the girl called out to her mother.

"Yes, baby," the woman said disinterestedly.

"Mumma, Mumma!" the girl continued.

"She will stand, it's alright," the mother said, pulling the child's hand and getting her down.

"Mumma, I want window!" the girl objected.

"No, Rhea. Please get down right now!" she persisted, pulling the girl's hand.

"Madam, it's no problem. Let her sit, it's no problem really. Besides her legs will ache," the man said with his dubious grin.

"No, it's ok, thank you." She held her daughter and picked her up from under her arms and placed her on the floor "Rhea, behave! Stand here. And hold on to that bar!" the woman said pointing to another joist.

She knew that her own mother would have whacked her up to standing in the same situation. However, the girl being an obedient child, didn't create further fuss about it all and stood holding on to the steel bar that ran from roof to floor and started tracing on the floral prints of another woman's dress who was standing next to her.

"Ok, madam. Ok, no problem," the man said plainly.

"But, thank you, sir," the woman replied, trying to repair any damage.

As soon as the announcement of the next stop came, the woman readied herself and her daughter to get down. The man gaped at them, wondering if it was actually their stop or she was getting down out of discomfiture. The man turned back to the window and continued to stare, lost in thoughts. Everyone was watching this in silence. And surely, they had all judged him by now. He watched the child prancing away through the window, her romper ends dangling as she jumped. Suddenly, the mother turned to him, saw him through the glass of the window that now separated them, and gave an expression of having caught him in some kind of an act. There was disgust in her eyes and she turned away and walked hurriedly in relief, pulling her daughter behind her. The man turned his back to the window as if nothing had happened and continued to stare at nothing like he had done on the platform.

The man got down at the next stop. He found a quiet spot on a lonely bench, took a moment, tied his shoes, and brushed his ruffled hair with the ends of his finger. He looked through the crowd of people, walking hurriedly, living the fast life. After some time, he got up to carry on and, on reaching the exit, realized that he had left his bag in the train. He rushed back in anxiety to get it back. To his relief, he found the bag and pulled it up against his shoulder again, this time holding it as if closer to his heart.

Just then, the same mother and her daughter got out of another train and, as she ran her eyes around to figure out the exit, she spotted him and was instantly terrified that he must be following them. She hid behind a pillar to watch him and followed his movements closely.

The man, seemingly unbeknownst, left the station and took the same lanes she was intending to take. *Does he know me? Has he been watching us all these days?* She had heard of such incidents as the same pool of people travelled every day. She trailed him as there was nowhere else to go, but home, dragging her obedient and now much-tired daughter, who having met the end of her train ride was disinterested. After what seemed like a long time, he took a turn into the road which led to the graveyard. The graveyard itself was small and in ruins. The life of the city seemed to die all of a sudden, the cool shades of the trees suddenly turned into dark, demonic avenues and even the sunlit struts of the leaves seemed to be consumed by ominous forces.

One end of the road was with garbage and opposite to it stood the entrance to a cemetery. The man walked into it, his head held down, the lace of his shabby shoes undone as he dragged it in the murk. The mother who was trailing stopped outside and watched the man through the collapsed walls of the graveyard. He turned to the first row, collapsed in front of a tiny tombstone, and began to cry like a child. He prostrated before it, his hands spread across the stone in an embrace, trying in vain to hold his dear one that lay buried there. He banged his fists on it and threw into fits of loud sobs. After a moment, he opened his bag and drew out a bunch of flowers, with the leaves still fresh and the mud on its surface still heavy. He muttered something, placed it on the tombstone, and kissed it. The mother looked at it closely. It said –

"In loving memory of Pari, beloved daughter. 1990-1995."

CAMOUFLAGE

I

"Do you think they will agree?"

"I don't know about mine, but yours will."

"Why not yours?"

"Because they are not really mine."

Kruthi just stood still as they reached the roots of the cashew tree. Yes, Parvati had a point; they were not really her parents.

"What color did the teacher say?" Parvati asked.

"Lavender."

"Never heard of it."

"It's just light purple."

"What did you say the name of your village was?" she asked as both of them flung their bags onto the muddy ground.

The upheaval of the afternoon dust revealed the air around. Parvati described again – her village, her parents, and everything she had left behind to come study in this remote colony set up by the state. Education was free here. She continued yapping. She knew Kruthi wasn't listening this time as well. But she talked anyway. The dust settled on their dry, naked legs. Their shoes had long lost the whiteness of their maker and had turned muddy brown. But nobody cared about the muddy shoes in a state-run school. They knew the families these children came from. Some were children of engineers, while others were of their assistants and helpers. So, they let it be. They didn't even care if they wore shoes or slippers. The uniform never maintained uniformity.

"Say, how do we tell them to buy us new shoes?"

"It's for the show! They HAVE to agree!"

"They don't have much of a choice?"

"No, they don't."

"Are you certain?"

"I am certain yours don't."

"Why not yours?"

"I told you, they are not really mine!"

"Oh! They will surely buy you a new pair! It's for the show!"

"Oh, I don't know."

They both briskly latched onto the roof of one of the deserted offices, over which the thickest branch of the tree hung itself in melancholy.

"Maybe you are right. They don't have much of a choice. Besides, look at these! They are already worn out! Even around the edges."

"Do you think we'd find them in lavender?"

"Oh yes, they come in all colors, I've seen them in the city."

"We can go to that store where Moocha sells shoes and check. We can go in the evening after milk!"

Kruthi was excited about her idea, and then mumbled slowly, "What will you do if they don't buy for you, Parvati? Will the teacher still allow you to dance?"

"I don't know," Parvati said meekly, her face turned pale as she thought about the imminent. "Lavender," she mumbled to herself. "Lavender, I don't know about, but I know how to turn this muddy brown to white!" she said chirpily, with a twinkle in her eyes.

"How?"

"You take a piece of chalk and then you rub it all over. After a while, you bang the shoes softly against a rock to let off the extra chalk dust"

"Where did you find the chalk?"

"I picked up the tiny last bits from the classroom floor. After everyone leaves and before the *aaya* comes to clean up."

"Oh! That's how your shoes are a bit whiter than mine! I should have known!" Kruthi's face gleamed with a smirk of having caught a thief.

Parvati was left embarrassed at Kruthi's tainty remarks. With disappointment about her thrifty cleverness having gone misinterpreted, she turned silent.

Kruthi plucked two of the juiciest-looking cashew fruits and carefully made her way down. She kept the bigger, juicier one to herself and gave the sour-looking one to Parvati. "You take this," she thrust it in her bag. Parvati soon forgot her disappointment and happily took the fruit, carefully placing it in her bag so as to not disturb the cashew nut that the fruit held.

"You know that new girl always has the whitest shoes. She was showing off that small bottle which she called something...po...po...*polees*," Parvati said.

"*Poleesh*. Papa has black *poleesh*. But it's in a small round tin and doesn't have a brush. So, he uses a separate brush to brush his shoes. It's called *poleesh*."

"Yes, yes! My uncle uses that too! I have seen him!"

"She is from the city."

"Yes, she smells so good every day. Even the teacher asked her how much soap she used while bathing to make her smell this good!"

Both of them slipped their feet into their shoes with their heels protruding outside the boundaries of the soles. They both frolicked away and once they reached Kruthi's quarters, they bid their byes, promising to meet in the evening to go to Moocha's shop to find out about the lavender dye for their shoes.

"I will talk to them, you do too." Kruthi waved to Parvati as she disappeared around the corner of the road.

II

That evening, Kruthi waited nonchalantly for her Papa to come home; her head rested on her palms as her elbows rested on the compound wall. She could see the other kids from the neighborhood playing with discarded tires. Her mother constantly prodded her as she sat behind her, combing her hair, brandishing its luxury as she did. "Why are you not out?" she prodded her again with the end of her comb. Kruthi didn't pay any attention. She wanted her mother to ponder over the reasons for her melancholy and prod her further. The more she pried about her melancholy, the better case she had.

Her friends called out to her often; you see, they were an odd number without Kruthi and failed to make teams without her. Though she was dying inside to just go and join them in their play, she put on a sorrowful face and continued to stare at them, feigning disinterest. Soon, her wait got intensely dreadful and spread to her limbs and fingertips. Her mouth began to dry. And seeing her friends and other kids continue to play without her, added to her weary. *What's taking Papa so long?* she thought.

"Go drink your milk!" her mother prodded her again as she flung her thick, black plait and rounded off all the fallen hair into a ball, and set it rolling like a tumbleweed into the mild wind. "It's already gotten cold."

Kruthi went stir-crazy and asked restlessly, almost yelling, "Why has Papa not come yet? I have to go to play with Parvati."

"So, go! Come back before it gets dark!"

"Why hasn't Papa come yet?"

"He must have gone to the dam; he was talking about a site inspection"

"Why didn't you tell me earlier!" she yelled at her mother again like everyone on the verge of adolescence does. That was the first time she had talked back to her mother. All the responsibility weighing on her tender shoulders made her realize the need to speak up for herself and her needs. She sprung like a deer awakened and gulped down her milk and dashed down the road to meet Parvati.

There was only one street in the entire colony that was commercial. At the beginning of the street was a small hotel that only had four items on its menu. Its façade was orange *peinture* with brown Mughal motifs. Next to it was a men's barber who had set up a petty shop with nothing but blue-painted planks. All the men and the kids of the colony, including Kruthi and Parvati, went there for a haircut. The barber and the hotel were thus unintended neighbors who always fought over their waste disposal. Whenever a customer found a hair strand in the food, the hotel manager blamed the barber.

"Do these bits of hair have wings that they will fly and come into your kitchen?"

"Look at the length of the hair! Do men have such long strands, it's surely Jaggamma's," he pointed at the cook.

Fortunately, today everything was quiet except Jaggamma who was scrubbing the utensils at the dead-end of the narrow bylane between the hotel and barber's. Kruthi and Parvati marched past her as they drew chips from a packet.

Next to it was Prakash Stores, the only grocery store and one-stop shop for household items for the entire colony. He lived in a town about 30 kms away and in a mansion, they said. He was the richest man the colony knew. And at any time of the day, one could find at least three kids leering over his glass-top counter to look at the candies from the city that were displayed for sale. Some screamed at their mothers, pulling the edge of their sarees to buy them one.

On any other day, Kruthi would do the same, struggling to get a glimpse of the candies. But not today. Today, for the first time, she felt much more than the wanting for candies; she had a bigger mission to accomplish. Honestly, this was the first time that either Kruthi or Parvati walked past Prakash Stores all by themselves to explore what lay beyond its limits. Next came a dingy shop which sold "cold drinks" and the children were told never to drink anything from there. Once they walked past it, they saw the big shop of Moocha. It had bales of cloth fabrics on display in one section and some shoes in the next section. In one of the rows in the footwear section, there lay the pricey small bottles, similar to the one that the new girl had flaunted. There were a range of colors.

Kruthi and Parvati looked at each other. They gleamed. It was the first time they had been to Moocha's without parents.

"Can you show us the lavender color *poleesh*?" Kruthi asked.

Moocha answered, his red lips watering around the sides as he chewed perpetually. Neither Kruthi nor Parvati could understand anything of what he was trying to tell.

"I don't think he himself heard what he said!" Kruthi said and they both giggled. "Say, why don't you spit it out!" she almost yelled at him "And show me the lavender *poleesh*!"

Moocha walked straight up to them jarringly and then stepped over them bending over Kruthi in an insolently unagreeable manner and spat out his tobacco and whatnot mixture into the gutter. She could smell the pungent thing and it hit her nose. She shook her hands in front of her nose to ward it off.

"There! I spit it out!" he said, "Forgive me, not many young children come around here, I forget my manners," he said with impudence. "Now again, there's no lavender polish. It comes only in black and white," almost immediately changing his tone.

"Then what's all that you have kept?" asked Kruthi who was unnerved by his effrontery.

"They are dyes. I have purple if you want."

"How much is it?"

"It will cost about twenty."

"Ok. I will bring the money"

They left the shop as soon as they could. Moocha bent over the counter and jeered at the girls.

It was getting dark.

"Twenty rupees!" Parvati exclaimed.

"Yes. I don't think you will be able to buy it. Don't ask your uncle or aunt."

"Why not!"

"*He* will not buy it for you. You are not their daughter that they would splurge so much money over a silly show of dance!"

Parvati's face sank.

"Once Papa buys it for me, I will share it with you."

Their conversation was drowned by a commotion over Jaggamma's unhygienic ways.

III

Papa was back by the time she reached home. The first thing Kruthi did was tap into her father's ego, "All the other parents are buying it! There would be no dance without the lavender shoes. Please, Papa, please. They will throw me out."

"Who will throw you out?" Papa was steering in the wrong direction.

"My teacher," she said hesitantly. She knew what Papa would suggest next. "You don't know how it feels! I will be embarrassed in front of everyone!"

"Who is this teacher? What's her name? I shall come and talk it out!" Papa was furious, "The stage is much higher and the audience below won't even be able to get a glimpse of your feet!"

"Papa, please. Everyone is getting it. It's an ensemble and shoes are an integral part of it. Whether the audience can see or not is not the question."

"So why don't you borrow some of the dye from one of your friends whose father has already bought them this thing?"

Kruthi turned furious, "You think I am Parvati? To beg, borrow from someone?"

"Aaaaha? Look at you! Not even stepping into teenage and throwing around so much air! Get out!" he threw her sullied shoes at her. But they narrowly missed her and banged against the railing outside the main door. Dust burst out of it and shone with all its minuscule resplendence against the sodium vapor street lamp that spread its rays through the interstices of the unperturbed yellow elder tree.

Kruthi knew this was coming, she picked up her shoes and then sat on the bench outside and sulked. She thought about crying to get more attention but was too furious at having talked about borrowing the dye from someone else. Does Papa have no pride? But that was how things worked in the colony, third graders passed down their textbooks to the second graders on the tenth of April every year, when annual exam results were announced. Some children held on to one particular senior and every year collected the handouts like a ritual and some ran around the roads in the evenings when all of them came to play and asked for their textbooks from them. And rarely, fathers arranged the books by seeking out their colleagues. These handouts would again be passed on to another deserving junior at the end of the next year. So, borrowing and passing on was not something unreasonable or unheard of. "But definitely not *poleesh* and dyes!" Kruthi concluded.

Kruthi grew despondent. How would she look in front of all her friends who have managed to get lavender shoes? She imagined herself alone offstage, singled out, with everyone jeering at her ragged, filthy shoes. She would be thrown out of the performance. Well, at least Parvati will be with her this time. Her foster parents would definitely not splurge on her. She quietly slid down the stairs and ran around the corner of the dark road to reach Parvati's house. And as she approached the gate, she saw Parvati's aunt smiling at her. "Parvati is not here, Kruthi. But she will be back in a while, you can wait if you want."

"Ok."

"Say, how's Parvati at school? Is she coping well?"

"Fine, Aunty."

"She's the shy kind. Doesn't open up to us much. But thank you for being such a good friend. She probably feels guilty about staying with us here."

"She's close to Mansi too, aunty."

"Yes, but she looks up to you mostly and whenever she talks, she talks about how you did this, how you did that."

"Oh, that's nothing."

Just then she saw Parvati trailing her uncle with a small brown bag in her hand. "There she is," her aunt exclaimed.

Parvati's aunt grabbed a small basket overflowing with vegetables from her husband afront the gate, not allowing him to enter the premises of the quarters. He immediately turned around and headed back the path he had just come from. And her aunt rushed back inside to cook, leaving the children to themselves.

"Look, Kruthi, uncle got me the dye!" Parvati was satisfied, with unfound happiness brimming over her face. Her place in the performance stood.

Kruthi's face shrunk. She stood in silence, staring at the brown bag Parvati was carrying.

"I am going to wash my canvas shoes now and soak them up in the dye-infused water. Hope it dries up well in a day or two. These rains are such a misery."

"Your uncle bought you the dye?"

"Yes. I was too reluctant to ask him, but then, he asked about the dance dress and if the tailor had it ready. I said yes. He then asked if I needed anything else, like bangles or matching hand bands. I said no. I have all those, right? In the end, I told him about the shoes and the dye in Moocha's shop. So, he took me immediately."

"Oh!" Kruthi was painfully shocked and surprised at this unexpected turn of events.

"There's enough dye in the bottle, we could use from this," she suggested.

"Haahahh," Kruthi chuckled nervously. "What are you saying! Papa has gone to the shop himself just now to bring it for me. I came by to ask if you wanted some!" she lied plainly, struggling to hide her big, fat failure. "I gotta go now."

A striking pain of humiliation pierced through the middle of her chest and swarmed all the tendrils of her nerves. *Parvati got it? She did? And I didn't? I didn't? But she did?* She raged into her house and her anger turned into a burst of tears in front of her father, who seemed to care lesser and lesser about the importance of the matter. He continued to count his sets on the dumbbells as he worked on his upper arms and back. "32, 33…" he continued, his ears not complying. But Kruthi continued to throw a fit. "Now everyone has got it! I will be thrown out by the teacher! I have to do as I am asked to and get the *poleesh* done for the show!"

Her father now took the yoga position of *sarvangasana* and breathed heavily to hold his position; his legs trembled in the air as blood rushed in his body.

"Fine!!" he screamed with his clenched eyelids. "Go and find out from the shop. How much is it?"

"It's twenty rupees"

"How do you know?"

"I already went and asked"

"You went past Prakash Stores? Did you ask your mother before going?" he seemed to be getting angrier with this enquiry.

"Yes, I did," she lied "and I was not alone; now come with me and buy it!" she commanded.

"Go and get it from Moocha. I need to see what product this is. Dye! I have never used or seen such a product to use as a substitute for polish."

"It's just to make the canvas shoes lavender."

"Just go and bring it"

And so, Kruthi wiped her tears and walked briskly past the same intermittent lights of the streets and reached Moocha's shop. The shadows had not shifted as she watched them grow bigger and smaller and then disappear and reappear from the light posts along her way.

"My Papa wants to see what the dye is and how it can be used or not used to color my shoes lavender," she said as her face flushed with embarrassment but tried to be vocal about her demand. It was but a strange request, she knew, and was expecting him to turn her away. She thought then she could directly skip over to the part where Dad would come and buy it already. Or even better just give her twenty rupees so that she can handle it from there herself.

To her surprise, Moocha grinned and handed her the tiny, flamboyant-looking bottle. She apologetically said that she would just show it to her father and bring it right away! *If Papa agrees, I would just come and throw a twenty rupee note on his face*, she thought. She ran her way back, each minute falling heavily on her conscience of having borrowed this bottle from the shopkeeper without having paid him a penny. She flashed it in front of her father, awaiting his examination and introspection.

Just then her mother came with a steel box filled with sambar and declared, "Kruthi, run along and give this to Bashyam uncle and come."

"No, Amma," she dismissed her mother's request and sat eagerly, watching her father for a reaction.

"Be a good girl, Kruthi. Bashyam uncle's wife left yesterday to her mother's. It will not take more than 5 minutes."

"But, *Amma*, I have to walk to the other side of the road!"

"Yes," she thrust the box into her hand. "He can just cook some rice and his dinner will be sorted."

"Everyone knows of the unhygienic Jaggamma's food. The poor man is suffering from so many ailments already! Get up!" she urged Kruthi.

"Not until Papa gives me twenty rupees for this."

She understood by her father's silence that she was pushing it. So, she grabbed the bag and walked out but not without giving a sideward glare at her examining Papa.

She hurried across the road and then through the small, dimly lit alley and barged open Bashyam's house. "Mother asked me to give this," she thrust it and before the man could offer his gratitude, she was gone.

"Just because he is from the same village as Mother, he thinks he will get free food every time that lady goes on holiday. To leave him like this and go so often! Mother never does that!" she mumbled as she walked back in the same dimly lit alley. A fleeting sense of pride about her mother crossed her mind.

Her father was waiting at the doorstep when she reached. He was holding out the dye bottle and said, "Now go and return this and come."

"But...but..." words failed her. Pertinence failed. What more should she do to get him to understand the importance? "You want lavender shoes, and you will get it. No part of your ensemble shall be compromised. Now, go and return this and come."

As she walked back alone, on the desolate road, her mind throbbed with the infinite possibilities of how her father could make such a thing happen. Did he have a friend from whom he could borrow? Would he ask her to share with Parvati? But she had already lied to her about it and it would be a great shame to go and belittle herself in front of her. *Oh! He's going to make me ask Parvati! Such a shame. Such a shame! How should I explain myself to her? I'd rather drop out of the show!* She reached Moocha's and as she drew the bottle of dye from the bag to return it, she saw a tiny driblet of dye had left a mark on the label and the seal of the bottle had been broken. The doer of this had tried to wash it away in vain. She hid the blob with her finger and returned it to Moocha, "I will not be needing this. But thanks." She turned around to a world where she now knew she'd have a lavender shoe. "But, such a shame!"

Migrant

The sun was already up in the sky and pierced the 60-year-old Prabhuram's skin as he stepped out of the cool shade of the green neem tree for a moment. Malli, his help, squatted at the trunk of the tree with a blank stare that followed his master as he loitered like an ant. They were waiting by the side of the state highway for the arrival of Prabhuram's sister and her son from the city. They were visiting after several years. The state highway was the widest and longest road the people of K-colony knew. It disappeared into the mists of the thick forests on either side and was their only tether to the outside world. Trucks loaded with cargo, sand, and vegetables passed occasionally. Sometimes the children stood on its muddy sidelines in awe of the size of the vehicles, for heavy vehicles plying were a rare sight in the colony.

Prabhuram was one of the very few who owned a small patch of land. He had grown many crops over the years, but over the last couple of years, only coconut trees were nurtured and harvested. The farm was about a 10-minute walk from where he stood and that was the nearest point where the bus would stop. There was no designated bus stop, and the driver only stopped if and when anyone waved his arm at the appointed place by the side of the road. It was the same for the buses that traveled in the other direction. Prabhuram wondered how his nephew would take his vacation in the colony as their life revolved around the small house nestled inside the farm. There was also a shed in the farm which was home to their two cows and one calf.

He looked up at the sky to check the weather. Innumerable sweat beads on his square face glistened under the afternoon light and a lot came together under cohesion and dripped off his perfect jawline. The cyclone in the neighboring coastal state had just begun to recede. And after a long week of melancholy, the sky had hoisted up a clear, blue color. There was not even a stray wisp of white. The heat felt sudden and stinging as if the skin had forgotten all about it. It was nearing noon. There was not a bird in sight. *Even they are escaping the heat*, he thought. Everything around him had turned green from the rains, but it was mostly weeds and creepers on big old trees. These would wither in a week or two under such sun. He looked in front of him on the other side of the highway and sat on a culvert gazing at the vast expanse of sear fields.

He turned to Malli who was now up and out in the sun. As he turned around, the appalling neon-green shirt he wore struck Prabhuram's eyes, and he was taken aback "What kind of color is that, Malli?! Didn't you find anything else?"

"My brother-in-law gifted me, *saukar*. He is a snake catcher."

"So he decided to dress you up like a pit viper? You and your ghastly shirts!"

"My wife would create a ruckus if I threw it out, *saukar*. Erm. You always wear white…I have noticed. It's always sparkling neat," he said, scratching his head.

"Yes, I like to wear only white," Prabhuram said dismissively, putting his gaze back on the endless highway.

Two trucks whizzed past Prabhuram, each vying to overtake the other. His tall figurine fell onto the dry mud as they grazed past him. He got up and yelled some curse words at them as he dusted off his broad shoulders. Malli dutifully repeated the same curse words at the drivers, picked a fistful of dirt, and threw it in their direction. After dusting off his shirt and lungi, Prabhuram checked his watch and sat on the milestone marker that read K-colony zero km, and below it was painted in black – Samjogi 45 kms.

K-colony was referred to as the "last village" by its oldest inhabitants and the natives. Nobody knew why it was referred to as the last village and with reference to what it was the last village. When an outsider asked any elderly resident why it was the last village they would simply reply, "What do we know of? You educated ones must know the answers to this." or "That was what my father and his forefathers to him have always told. And that is what I have told my son." There was a coppice on the outskirts of the colony beyond which there lined up rows of huge trees of an unusual kind. The elderly always fantasized it as a topographical oddity considering the fact that the colony was relatively a flatland. Stories were told about how Lord Rama planted those trees for vantage when he traveled south and that beyond it had spread a wide lake, as large as the mountains itself. It had all dried up now of course. And for this, Prabhuram was proud of his village. It's not just any other village on your map, he'd say.

Waiting didn't feel like waiting at all. Because time was slow even when there was no waiting to be done. So it was another chore. Prabhu sat chewing nothing and occasionally gnawed his teeth to bite the remains of the areca nut in his mouth. Malli just did what his master did, and it began to get on Prabhu's nerves. His fixated eyes spotted the familiar, ostentatious bus that suddenly appeared from afar. The pom-poms and woolen *jhumars* danced up and down as it thumped into unwelcome potholes and unplanned speed-breakers. Prabhuram got up from where he was sitting and waved his arm as the zany bus neared him slowly. The driver stopped as if he knew beforehand where to stop and a saree-clad woman and a curly-haired boy in ripped jeans and t-shirt got down from it. Soon, the bus veered off impatiently and resumed its show on the highway, leaving behind only smoke and dust.

"Come, Shanta, come. Why is the bus late today?"

"Oh Ramanna, the tire got punctured and they took forever to change it"

"How are you, Lohitha? Studies?"

"Lohith!" the boy replied quietly but sternly. They started walking along the path that led to the house. "Careful, son," his mother warned him.

"Malli, take the bags."

"Yes, *saukar.*"

"I thought you'd missed the point of alight. It has been so long!"

"No, Ramanna, how can I forget the house where I grew up!" Shanta said as she smeared her hair with her greasy hands.

"It's just… they say the city changes rapidly. I cannot recognize the street that leads to your house when I come to the city. Change is very slow here," Prabhuram said.

"More like change has never arrived," Lohith muttered.

"But the fields change too. The plants and bushes overshoot, the blooms are different and the rustle of the winds variegated."

As they reached the coconut grove, Shanta gasped in surprise at the crumbling state of the plantation in front of her, "What happened to these coconut trees, Ramanna? I can barely recognize it!"

The smell of wet hay from the cowshed struck the air, too familiar and welcoming for Shanta and Prabhuram. But Lohith cringed and covered his nose with the torso of his t-shirt. Malli was walking too closely to Lohith and this annoyed him. He waved his hand in the air as if to drive away the flies and drove Malli to maintain some distance between them.

Three big piles of dried coconuts lay heaped in the sun next to the cowshed. "You should really put it all out in the sunlight for some more time," she said, concerned about their poor treatment, "And where have you put the rest of it?"

"Rest of it?! This is all we got this year!" his face turned sad instantly. "Unseasonal rains and infestation ruined one-third of the produce."

"This is not even half of what we used to get back then!"

"Yes. And I don't know how much of this will give good marketable copra."

"They seem alright from the outside," Shanta reassured.

"Yes. They all do. They always seem alright from the outside, just like your husband!" his warm tone of hospitality when he had received them seemed to have come to an end. "Now, why don't you go in and freshen up? We will talk later."

As she entered the unventilated veranda of the house, Shanta stumbled for a second as sudden darkness set onto her eyes. She stared into the darkness, her face stoic with the thought of her husband.

"Come in, Lohitha," he said to the boy patting his back "How you have grown up so soon!" "Katyayini! Come. They are here," he called out to his wife to receive his sister. "Malli, go and keep the luggage inside the first room"

"Who is this man?" Shantha whispered to Prabhuram as Malli disappeared behind the curtain of the first room.

"He is Mallinath. He has come from the northern district and lives with his wife and child in the lookout hut."

"Look, Lohith, the floor is so cool despite the heat. I will sit on the floor." She rubbed her hands on the cool red-oxide flooring that had given way at many places to create potholes of cement dust.

"Do whatever pleases you," Lohith says, disinterested.

Everybody was served a glass of jaggery water and it spread like wild ice into their system. Lohith left his glass carelessly in the middle of the room and left to examine the small garden and its creepers in front of the porch. After a moment he returned, slipped his sandals, and furthered into the aerated soils of the coconut grove. Malli squatted and sat on the porch outside. His eyes followed Lohith with his mouth open in astonishment at this city boy.

As the sun lowered, everyone gazed at the dust in the sunlight that fell into the veranda. And there was pity and sadness in their eyes at the bad state of the coconut trees.

"You should really get the manure and pesticides sprayed over it soon. The gum is secreting on the trunk. See there, some have developed spots too." She pointed her fingers at a group of trees.

Worry filled his heart. Like every other farmer, for Prabhuram, the earth was dear to his heart and the crops had been something of his creation, his only asset. To see the magic of his hands not working anymore and to see the deterioration of his land under his own eyes disheartened him.

"I know, I know! You think I can't see all that? Everyone has left, Shanta. It is not like how it was before. Nobody wants to work in the farm anymore. Things have changed. They are going to the city. Construction and other such labor give them better wages. *Sigh*. What am I to do alone? That Manju left last month. I have brought some help from the neighboring village. I have them for now, but I know they will not stick around for long either, just like the ones before them."

"Manju left?!"

"Yes. Not just that, he took Rajanna along too."

"What… what do you mean he took him along?"

"Oh, where should I begin! Someone from the city wrote to him of these opportunities, made it sound so rosy and that if he was willing to come, he could do something for him too. Manju confided in Rajanna about his thoughts of leaving the village. And when Rajanna heard of it, he wanted to go too. Almost begged Manju to take him. They all think the city helps them lay golden eggs. Idiots, all of them! Let them go! Let them all go, I don't need such men for my plantation!" He hated the city like it were a witch trying to seduce his dear ones away. Things were slipping out of his hand. "First my sons left, then my health and all that with the surgery, then came the coconut yield, and now the laborers! They have worked in our fields for almost twenty years. How could they leave!"

"They were the only ones that loved the plantation like it was their own. The trees need love and compassion as much as they need manure and pesticides. Anybody can spray, but to shower love is not everyone can do. As long as

I am alive, I shall put my blood and sweat into nurturing them."

Abandonment filled the air.

Just as Lohith returned from his stroll, Katyayani brought a plastic tray of bowls. "Here."

"What's it, *Attige*?"

"The first milk. Gauri gave birth last Tuesday. I have some first milk left. Give Lohith too, it's very nutritious."

"Colostrum. Yuck. I don't want it." Lohith looked away, his face distorted in disgust.

"Well, What do you know, son! It will do good to your heart and bones. Have a little."

"Absolutely not. Where is the bathroom? I need to freshen up. This mud is creeping upon me."

"It's your soil. Mother will always hold on to her own. Go down the corridor, get down the steps and it's to your left," Prabhu said.

Lohith returned, sat beside his mother and whispered into her ears, "The bathroom is so old, *Amma*, there's just a separation built like a mound that holds the water tank and they don't even have hand sanitizer."

Shanta ignored him.

"Then how did you get these coconuts harvested?"

"Malli. He is the only help left. Reliable. Follows my instructions but is not as knowledgeable as Rajanna. Girija, his wife, helps too, both in the fields and with the household. He is sending his daughter to the government school here. When the colony was formed they set up a school too, as the children of the families that were posted here needed education." Even as he was talking to Shanta, his eyes wandered off to Malli, who was now busy drawing up a drain in the ground for water to flow around the field.

"Make sure those stones and stray grass are removed" he shouted across the field to Malli.

"*Haan, saukar*!" Malli agreed faithfully. He continued work around the culvert like he was built to do it. He didn't lift his eyes up even momentarily to check his surroundings or to take a break. He had forgotten to check Lohith too whom he had relentlessly pursued throughout the day.

"If the water clogs, it will overflow everywhere!" Prabhu shouted across again.

"*Haan, saukar*!" he said in a muffled voice as his head was still bent, working tirelessly over the culvert.

Everyone lost track of time in the humdrum discussions. For Shanta, it was a time of catharsis, as she poured out her difficulties at the hands of her husband, but kept the darkest secrets within herself. It was the same for Prabhuram as he lamented the state of affairs in his village. Soon, the evening sunlight fell on the white cows in the cowshed and they turned golden. Dusk fell on the colony and it brought with it the chirping of the home-bound birds. Katyayani brought some tea for everyone and placed a separate one for Malli, who was returning towards the house, on a concrete bench outside. Malli's daughter ran across the farm, joined by some other children for an evening game. She occasionally looked at her mother for approval of each of her actions during the game, as Girija sat outside the hut combing her oiled, black hair.

Malli cleaned up all the tools and put them in their place beside the small garden. "What is this?" Lohith asked Malli.

"That's the black pepper creeper," Malli said earnestly, standing with crossed hands and slightly crouched shoulders. His white dhoti had gathered dust and sweat and a red cotton towel hung around his bent shoulders as he tried to hide his naked torso.

"Take the tea, Malli?" Katyayani called out.

"No, *Amma*. Girija will be waiting."

As the boy went ahead to hold the small green pepper drupes in his palm, Malli went ahead and plucked one or two and extended it to the boy. "Here, *Anna*, smell it," he said, crushing it. "It's not for selling, but by the end of the year, *Saukar* gets to use it in his kitchen. But first, you have to dry it well. Here, smell it, *Anna*. It's very strong. Be careful." He thrust it to Lohith's face.

"Ummm, yes. God! That's strong."

"These are betel leaves, and over there are some tomatoes, lemon, and chili plants." He bent sidewards, lifting up his fingers to point to the backyard. "There stands a jackfruit tree too," he said, excited about all they had on the plantation. He felt happy that the hip city boy was finally talking to him. Malli had worked long enough now to know everything about the plantation. A sense of fondness filled his face as he went about it all.

"*Maama* doesn't need to go to the market ever, I believe."

"No, *Anna*. In fact, if anything goes to the market from here, it's these coconuts."

"Hah!"

"What are you doing in the city, *Anna*?" Malli asked Lohith curiously.

"I am studying Engineering. Just started."

"Oh," Malli's eyes brightened up. "I have a daughter, she is in class four. She is very bright. All her teachers say she is very clever too. She brings good marks, or so they tell."

"That's very good."

"You see, *Anna*, there? That's our hut. She studies all evening before the sun sets, making the best use of light. Then she comes over here to *Saukar's* porch where there is a bulb and studies till dinner. Poor girl. She works very hard."

"Good. Good."

"How is the city, *Anna*?"

"It's good. Much different from how it is here."

"I have never seen the city. Only once many years back. In my head, it is always filled with light and the sound of the rich. Big people, important people. No?"

"Yes. But there are various kinds of people. Not just big and important ones."

"Oh?"

"Yes. There are people like you too. Lots of them."

"Are there good schools there, *Anna*?" he asked eagerly.

"Yes, many of them. There are schools to get you into schools too!"

"Oh?" he exclaimed, bewildered at a strange practice.

"Yes."

"It must be a better life. How is…"

"*Ay!* Malli!" Prabhuram yelled dourly from where he sat. He had heard the entire conversation. His outburst nipped Malli's enthusiasm.

"*Haan, saukar*? *Haan*?" said a startled Malli, as if woken up from a trance. He ran towards his master in close steps, even though he was just a few feet away.

"Go check on the cows, feed them, and lock up the shed," Prabhuram said with all authority and banishment.

"*Haan, saukar*. Right away." Malli dashed in a hurry, with no further delay.

As soon as he was done, Malli gathered his playing daughter and disappeared into the darkness across the field to his tatty hut. The tea meant for Malli had turned cold. The floating milk skin broke into pieces like a parched piece of earth.

Prabhuram closely followed Malli with his eyes until he reached his hut. He then turned to Shanta. "This year, come again for Dusshera!"

"No, Ramanna, his father will not allow it. He says you have to light a lamp at your own house first on the festival day." Her face again turned stoic, with a sense of uneasiness prevailing over her, a small smile froze on her face as an act of show.

"Ah, yes. He is right," her brother agreed.

The Man with the Blue Wagon-R

On that new moon day, I returned home rather disturbed and concerned. I did not want to bump into that man again, so I rushed through the stairs. I ran through the corridors and rang the doorbell repeatedly until Yuvaan took to the door. He was taking such an unusually long time to open up! I shut the door with a thud and slung my mule slippers wildly.

"That man is troubling me," I declared my trouble. It was too much to take now!

"Who?"

"That man with the blue Wagon-R"

"What did he do?"

"He's causing me trouble wherever I go."

"What did he do?"

"He follows me wherever I go"

"Where had you been?"

"Market, parking, on the road when I go for a walk, common area, he follows everywhere."

"Just ignore him."

"He drives past me whenever I go out."

"So?"

I'm 50 and my hair has turned gray. I color my hair, which my sister finds "unnaturally black". She says I use an outdated brand and that "Your age shows on your face." That's what she thinks. This place is not up to our standards. All kinds of people stay here, but it did not appear so when we moved in. When we moved in there was a public park where we would take a stroll in the evenings and the sound of the children filled my heart with joy. At least it did on some days it did. The park is long gone now.

Yuvaan asked me to calm down and move on. He doesn't understand. And I know what he thinks. He thinks what is to become of it? After all, I am an old woman and unattractive. But this is not an isolated incident. He doesn't understand how women get bothered by men and their behavior. Their ogling and its cues.

At night as we sat at the dinner table, I tried to tell him again. He asked me the details of the man, if I had known him or seen him before, which block he lived. After dinner, he went out for a stroll, said he needed fresh air. But I knew he went to deal with that man with the blue Wagon-R. I knew it because he is not the kind who takes night strolls.

When he returned, his face was grimaced and he went right to bed. My heart had not known peace, and sleep had evaded my eyes for so long, but that night I felt a tiny bit of comfort. I did not see that blue Wagon-R the next day and a week after that. It was obviously Yuvaan's doing. He knew how to deal with such people.

The next week, as I rolled the *chapathis* in the kitchen, humming the tunes of Ilayaraja, I was startled by the roaring sounds of a motorbike. The kind that the mechanics do in the workshops to quality check. There was no workshop around that place, so I looked out the window to see what it was all about. A man in a red shirt went on and on revving a bike by the side of the road. He looked up, studying the houses and his eyes fell on me. My panic set in. This was a man sent by the man with the blue Wagon-R and he knew everything about me, my past. That I am a dishonorable woman. That I'm looking for something or someone beyond my man and my marriage. Let me tell you, all of it is fabricated! These men are spreading false things about me. They want to ruin me! I immediately shut the window and ran inside to the corner bedroom. I could see the empty pan searing on the stove, but the revving continued for a good fifteen minutes.

After much time elapsed, I gathered some old newspapers and tape, and went back to the kitchen. As I taped the newspaper to the window glass, the pregnant woman from the opposite block walked out to put her laundry up in the balcony. She waved to me every day as I stood there cooking dinner or cleaning the platform. Yet, despite knowing that I was at my kitchen window, she did not even look at me as I cut out newspapers to the window pane size. Why do you think she would do that? A perfectly friendly person who has been exchanging niceties for so long suddenly stops talking today. I'll tell you why. These men have been spreading false rumors about me and she too has been told these things about me. That was the reason the man was revving his bike. To let me know "we know everything about you and so do your friends and family".

After a while of putting up the newspapers and shutting down all the curtains, the revving started again. Like I told you, it's their way of saying that they will not stop at anything, not even if I bring iron curtains down on my house. And despite my efforts to remain unseen, they will pull my name in the murk. Now, how do I explain this to Yuvaan? He would not believe me. He would not believe me if I told him that the friendly pregnant lady stopped talking to me today. All he says is 'ignore'. But pray tell me, how can a woman ignore such maligning, such injustice? All week he's been after me saying things like, "You stop pretending! You loiter around the corridor and windows as if to catch an unintended glimpse! You are always lurking in the balcony!" Or "Go and do something useful, occupy yourself, and don't think too much about it." As if I have been inviting all this misery in my life.

But I *know* that every time I "try to do something else", there is a stalker out there, outside my door who is telling wrong and untrue things about me to the entire community, to defame me. I know this because, even as I hole up myself inside my bedroom, there's a number of bikes whirring past on the main road. I lashed out at Yuvaan for not doing enough, not confronting the man with the blue Wagon-R or these other people. But all he does is take strolls after dinner on some nights and somehow the revving of the bikes stop and the blue Wagon-R man doesn't bother me for a while. I can prove it even now, if I step out for a while all eyes are going to be on me.

However, in the meanwhile, I did what Yuvaan suggested I do. I really did. Every evening the ladies of the quarters came and sat in their balconies sipping their teas as they kept a mindful eye on their children who played down on the roads. So that evening, I put effort, tweezed my eyebrows, cleaned up nice, took out my favorite checkered silk saree and draped it to perfection. I used my old, red vermillion paste and placed a rather large, round circle with it on my forehead, like I did in my younger days. I plucked a rose and clipped it to the side, behind my right ear. I uprooted a Windsor chair out of its pair and placed it outside on the other side of the L-shaped balcony where the landing of the stairs was clearly visible.

I sat down with my cup of tea in direct view of the window of the other block. There lived a big family of an elderly couple and their married sons and grandchildren. The elderly lady had always been fond of me. She would peep through her curtain and look at me every time I was in the balcony, and especially in the evenings when I dressed up nice. Following that she would complement me when we would meet in the common area, "I loved your saree yesterday, so beautiful! Bright colors! And even your jewelry!" or "You have such a lovely face too!" She usually did so out of her own accord.

But today, I wanted to chat. So I called out to her and she came to her window. That way, *those* people would know that they cannot deter me or my spirit. I told her how wonderful the markets this season were and that she must go visit. I noticed she was rather distant today, but she asked me about my hair. "When I was young, I had the thickest hair. My mother had the hardest time maintaining it. Each braid was *this* thick," I made a circle the size of a muskmelon with my palms. "All the girls envied my hair." She seemed not so distant after that. Perhaps the gossip had reached her too, but she changed her mind about me after I talked to her. I loved my younger days.

Suddenly I knew that it was the hour for *that* man to return and I rushed back inside rather abruptly. I shut down the sliding doors and drew all the curtains. That night the bikes roared, plying on the roads up and down like never before. *He* must have seen me in the evening. I just knew it. And that he had assumed that I had dressed up for him. I was so anguished! Yuvaan wouldn't believe a word of what I had to say. I thought about talking to my sister, but I knew she wouldn't believe me either. My sister would take joy in my plight, she was always jealous of me growing up, as did everyone I knew. Also, I didn't want to cause anyone distress. Yuvaan hardly talks to me these days and says all I talk about is the man with the blue Wagon-R if he ever did try to talk to me. And I can understand. No man would want his wife to talk about another man all day, even if it is in bad light.

The next day I could not get out of bed and stayed there till late afternoon. Yuvaan had left for work. He didn't disturb me either or that's what he claimed. Maybe because he knew it would get overwhelming if he even simply tried to talk to me. I sulked in bed, feeling depressed, hopeless and helpless. I felt cornered and nobody believed me. All day, I wondered if the man with the blue Wagon-R saw me from where I sat in the balcony. I thought maybe I laughed too much and held my chest too high and seemed very happy. And *he* thought these to be "gestures", an invitation.

It sickened me and my head banged like recoiling barrels from inside. I pulled out my cashmere shawl and covered myself in its entirety. I wanted to disappear. And he should not be able to spot me anywhere. That rogue! I did not go out of the house all week. I was not interested in cleaning up or cooking which I usually did. My hair turned gray again and my face was always greasy. I screamed and yelled at Yuvaan over anything he said or wanted.

"You can't stay indoors all the time," Yuvaan said on Saturday afternoon, "Come, let's go for a drive." I was not interested but when he persisted, I said I would come only after sunset and after it got dark enough. He tried to assure me that he was there with me, but I couldn't take any chances. And by seven in the evening, I gathered my cashmere shawl and sneaked out to the car. We drove and drove for a long time. It was not until we reached the outskirts that I rolled down the window.

Yuvaan stopped outside a garden that had rows of shops all lit up for the festivities. We bought some snacks and sat down on the ledge by the side of a small hotel. We enjoyed our snacks, with Yuvaan talking about his work, his boss being hard on him, and the stress he was under to complete the project. I was barely able to listen or think what to say to him. My head ached constantly and I had this compulsion to clench my teeth. I had no words of solace for him. His problems didn't seem important or pressing. I was just about to tell him that when a blue Wagon-R drove past us. Even before I said something, Yuvaan turned to me like lightning. He jumped as if something frightful had struck him. He knew! Why would he look otherwise?

"Look! He's here too!" I shrieked, "You see now, don't you? Please let's get out of here. Please!" I begged Yuvaan.

I went and sat inside the car. All the people around were looking at me in disgust. They knew! Everyone knew of me! Another man spat at the side of the road, pretending to spittle out his *paan*, but I knew, in actuality, he was spitting on me. Terrified, I cried. What can I do to make this stop? But Yuvaan denied everything and failed to acknowledge what was clearly there for him to see.

"So, what if it's a blue Wagon-R? There are hundreds of them out there. Sometime back I saw a white one. You didn't notice. It's unreasonable what you are expecting!" Yuvaan said on the way back.

"You don't want to believe me. Here I am, pouring my woes and asking you to help. But instead, you side with *those* men." Another roaring bike rumbled past us.

Yuvaan took me to a psychiatrist after that. I did not talk as a protest. Yuvaan went on and about narrating to the doctor. "She gets hysterical," he finally said as a closing statement. It was all sounding like I was making it all up. He said I was imagining things and the doctor asked me a few questions to which I nodded rather disengaged. *To hell with him*, I thought. I knew very well that the word had spread and the doctor too was also a part of this. He prescribed some pills or so Yuvaan said turning to me. Like a lawyer, he pleaded the doctor's case and said that I should take the pills three times a day without fail.

As soon as we came out, he turned to me finally and said, "Did you understand what the doctor was trying to tell you? It's a disorder."

I was disgruntled. "I don't know how to make you believe me. It's unbelievable! Did you not notice that peon who came in when we were talking?"

"Yes, so?"

"So? He was wearing a red-checkered shirt"

"So what?"

"It means that the man and the doctor and everyone here knows of me too. They all here think I am a woman of lost cause."

Yuvaan grew impatient, "So tomorrow if I wear a red shirt and buy a blue Wagon-R, what will it mean?"

He was not willing to understand or was trying to deliberately pretend to not understand like he had done in all these years of our marriage. He would hardly speak but he understood my intent.

The pills, I threw them all out.

After a couple of days, Yuvaan came up with the idea that I should spend some time at my sister's. A change of air. She was all I had now. She was unaware of all this trouble I was going through and I wondered if she would be empathetic to my situation if I confided in her. She was a woman after all. I could see the relief in Yuvaan's eyes as he dropped me off. He told my sister that I was going through a phase of hysteria and maybe something to do with the hormones. And that I could use some friendly company.

At Vinita's, I spent most of my time in the reading room. The house had two helps, one young girl and a man they had newly hired to do all the chores and he was also their driver. Whatever I needed, the girl brought it to me. In the morning I sat in the lawn to get some sunlight, as suggested by Vinita. In one corner of the land was a small room, presumably for the driver to sleep. On the first day, I thought he was looking at me and I said so to my sister. She didn't bother. The next morning as I walked about on the dew drops on the grass, there he was, that helper, trying to hawk up a loogie, the door to his room ajar. Now, I am quite familiar with this practice, but the man did it so repeatedly that it cracked up my nerves. I went in and talked to my sister about it.

"You know why he is doing that, don't you?" I asked her.

"Who? The driver?"

"Yes. Him. He joined recently, didn't he? Didn't you say so? What did he tell you about me?"

"He didn't say anything about you. He doesn't know you," she giggled in amusement. Oh, she had not changed, that bitch! She stood there, completely reveling in my misery.

"You are a part of this, aren't you?" I looked at her in disgust. Of course, she knew!

"He does it every morning, Anita. This is not new. It's disgusting, I will give you that! But what can I say!"

He was making obscene gestures with his door open. You know the meaning of an open door, don't you? And my poor little sister claimed she didn't understand what the man was trying to do! How ridiculous! This went on for a couple of days; there were delivery boys, the grocery man, the milkman, the vegetable vendor, and many more. I was swarmed by these people wherever I went. At times I felt trapped but I was not the one to bog down!

The next week I heard Vinita talk to Yuvaan over the phone. She talked in hushed tones and I knew what she was on and about. She sent the girl to the pharmacy and then I knew when the milk tasted bitter. But I was told to drink it. Yuvaan rang me up and commanded I just drink it! And that I was making everybody's life hell. I didn't know *when* I dozed off. It was the evening of the next day when I woke up. I felt a bit lighter and drowsy. I could hear my sister talk on the phone again, "Such a pity, she has everything in life. A beautiful family, money, absolutely no qualms. And to lead such an ungrateful life despite it all is really a shameful play of fate." She probably was genuinely concerned. I cannot say. I don't know what to think of anyone anymore.

Yuvaan came to pick me up the next day. I just listened to him going on and on about why I was being like this, and that I was doing it all intentionally. He asked about the pills again and I said I wouldn't take them. He screamed at me, one hand on the wheel and the other in the air, "You have turned our home and my life into a ghetto. You must and should take it or I will have to thrust it down your throat myself."

Upon reaching home, I went straight up to the terrace and stood with the cashmere covering my entire face. I once loved the ocean; we live by the ocean but now I hate the color blue. I am going to burn all things blue. They are a constant irritant to my eyes and I just cannot stand them. The man with the blue Wagon-R must be staring at me from his window. A perverted rejoice.

www.ingramcontent.com/pod-product-compliance
Lightning Source LLC
LaVergne TN
LVHW090929150826
845672LV00006B/1448

* 9 7 9 8 8 9 1 8 6 7 6 6 6 *